Rabbit Pie

RABBIT PIE

BRIAN CLEMENS

Introduction
by
Stephen Gallagher

CONTENTS

FOREWORD

AN INTERVIEWER ONCE ASKED ME WHAT I DID TO relax between writing assignments, I told him "I write"! So, faced by a hiatus between commissioned works, I decided to scribble a few short stories.

I grew up reading Maugham, Collier, Saki, O. Henry *et al*, have always loved the format, mourn its decline and am aware that many have been the original source of some wonderful movies—from *Stagecoach* to *Rear Window*. My stories have been good to me, threatened with publication on several occasions, something has always intervened to keep them safe.

Nevertheless, in the interim, two were adapted for TV and a third—though not actually made—was commissioned to screenplay, earning me (and this was back in the Seventies) in excess of £40k! And since then another story has been mooted as a stage play. Nice to feel one is still moving forward.

—*Brian Clemens, August 2013*

INTRODUCTION

YOU PROBABLY THINK YOU HAVE A HANDLE ON BRIAN Clemens. I know I did. Ingenious and prolific writer of tense screen narratives, trained in the hard school of postwar poverty-row film-making. One of the first and arguably the greatest of British TV's showrunners, long before the term was even invented. The man whose stamp on *The Avengers* transformed a modest Saturday-night drama into a global '60s phenomenon. Creator of *The Professionals*, author of forty-three (*43!*) standalone feature-length teleplays over six seasons of *Thriller*. For a little variety he created a BAFTA award-winning sitcom in *My Wife Next Door*.

Let's not even try to count the number of episodes he wrote for series he didn't create, both in Britain and during several spells in Hollywood, invariably turning in work that raised the bar for other contributors. We'd be here forever, look them up. We haven't even touched on the feature work yet. Writer/director of the true cult classic *Captain Kronos, Vampire Hunter*. Collaborator with the legendary Ray Harryhausen on *The Golden Voyage of Sinbad*. Purveyor of smart twists on the emper-illed-heroine thriller in *And Soon the Darkness* and *Blind Terror* (aka *See no Evil,* and a personal favourite of mine).

Most writers specialise. A few get to diversify. Clemens has done it *all.*

Or perhaps not quite. At least, that's what I thought.

When he agreed to write the introduction to my own first collection of short stories, I was cock-a-hoop. I'd always considered him a role model. And while knowing that I'd never achieve his dizzy output, I thought that here, for once, I was making a mark in an arena that he'd never entered. The Fontana paperback versions of his *Thriller* stories had been adapted for publication by Ted Hart, and I took this as a sign that his interests stopped short of short fiction.

The fact that you're holding this volume means one thing for certain; you know more on the subject now than I did then.

In fact, Clemens began writing short stories in childhood and, according to various sources, saw his first in print at the age of twelve. It appeared in the Hospital Saturday Fund magazine and he was paid a guinea, making it his first professional sale. In interviews he's referred to short fiction as a good training ground for a television writer. He'd go on producing it well into his screenwriting career.

The stories in *Rabbit Pie* may be relatively early work, but they're the real thing. In his short fiction Clemens shows the same skill and flair to be found in all of his writing. These are tight, well-crafted and satisfying stories, told in a variety of voices by a varied range of characters—some lovable, some less so, some downright appalling, all heading for that unexpected last-page fate that may raise a smile or a wince or a gasp before you're drawn on to the next.

You may recognise elements or themes that were to reappear else-where. The underlying premise of *Tattoo*, for example, would later drive an episode of *Hammer House of Mystery and Suspense* (but only the premise; the handling is very different). The stories in the collection stand alone and this edition, as far as I'm aware, is the only place where you can find them brought together. Mentions of earlier Clemens collections are like fleeting internet ghosts, impossible to hunt down, yielding nothing corporeal at the end of the chase.

In which case this collection also becomes the document of record, the first reliable reference for anyone wishing to study the short fiction written over Brian's long career. Times may change and new taboos replace the old, but to rewrite our history is to render it inauthentic. When pulling together previously-uncollected material it's important to honour the sources, and that's what the author and his publisher have done.

After being a lifelong fan, interviewing him twice on film festival stages, and working alongside him when we were both story consultants on the BBC's technothriller series *BUGS*, I thought I pretty much knew all there was to know about Brian Clemens.

Whatever you think you know, there's always more.

—*Stephen Gallagher, August 2013*

RABBIT
PIE

This could be both my debut *and* my swan song ... so there's a lot of 'em!

Jan (the bestest of all)

Sons, Sam and George

My dearest friends, Ron and Pat Westcott

Sir Alfred Hitchcock

All at Oval Road School

The Bar Pedro & Co, Raymond and Wendy (the best of aristos)

Lord Grade (Miss you, Lew)

Fred Astaire

Mrs Calabash wherever you are

Patrick MacNee (a true gent, even truer friend)

Albert Fennell, (who taught me the movie business, the kindest unsung hero I ever knew)

Mark Twain (relatively speaking)

Anthony Wedgwood Benn

Ray Greenfield and his idol, Vic Oliver

Edward Pugh

Corporal Stigant and his infallible wallet

Ivor, my dear old brother who I hope finally found his winner

Jo Lumley

June Randall

Caroline Munro and her Charley bars

Miles Mascard, master craftsman

Gareth Hunt

Bob Fuest (painter's director)

Brennie (remember when?)

Daphne, the old broad

Big Marge and Brother Groves

Sue and all the Holdernesses and Pipers

Diane Margot E

Laurie Johnson (great friend and composer extraordinaire)

Maureen and Peter

Susan and Old Arsey (we love him really)

Enzo Ferrari's song. Of the twelve.

Michael and Lesley (Ivor's best production)

Fil (much missed, never forgotten)

Mike and Doff Thompson

John Ford

John Sturges and Sam Peckinpah (How the West was won!)

Woody Allen and Groucho Marx

El Cortijo Viejo and all who sailed in her

Richard Bates (who gave my humour full rein)

B Bop's 1 & 2—Tilly and Carol

Gabby Drake (some pussy cat)

Sandy and Somerset Moore

Ewan (my finest pupil) and luvly Leanne

Ann and Ash of India

The Mortons and the Parrish mob

John Hough

Ian Gibbon

Mo Scully and Tower Bridge!

Arsene Wenger

Billy Wilder

And of course, my late, great, never to be forgotten mate and occasional co-writer, Dennis Spooner. Not a day goes by I don't miss you mate—and I keep the tea cosy standing by for you to wear anytime.

George Going Home

GEORGE LEANED AGAINST THE TINTED GLASS OF THE penthouse suite, looked out across the Hudson River and saw Sheffield. Far, far below the rumble of traffic drifted up from Fifth Avenue but George heard only the muted roar of the iron foundry, and the distant bleat of sheep on the moors.

"Mr. Killick?" George was brought back to the present by the diffident voice of his secretary, "Mr. Killick the car is waiting." George nodded and picked up his brief case and the few paper backs he had selected at the drug store that morning; "Bon voyage, sir," she pursued him to the door, ". . . and be sure to relax, rest, you certainly deserve to."

Outside, under the awning of The Killick Building, Frank stood immaculate in his pearl grey uniform that exactly matched the grey of the long, stretch out limousine. As George appeared Frank opened the door of the car for him, but then George stopped and looked back at the building and wondered one more time whether, or how, they would get along without him. Then he put it behind him and climbed into the car. Unless George had clients in the car, entertaining them with the closed circuit television, or with drinks from the cocktail cabinet, he usually kept the glass division down. So that he could talk to Frank. Frank was one of the very few of his employees who did not treat him with tongue-tied awe, Frank would always chat happily about everyday things, and frequently took George's mind off the grimmer business of tycoonery. Today was no exception, "It must feel kind of crazy, eh, sir?"

George smiled, "Crazier than that."

"I mean," Frank continued, "Going back after all these years, how long is it?"

"Forty years, Frank." Yes, it was almost exactly forty years since George's family had packed up and come to America, since then he *had* been back, yes to London perhaps a hundred times, but never to his home town, never with enough time to go there. "How old were you when you left, sir?"

"Fourteen." Fourteen, a frightened, skinny boy with a Yorkshire accent you could cut with a knife, and of which faint traces still remained, in the vowel sounds mostly, remained to amuse and enchant his friends.

"Well, you've certainly come a long way since then, sir."

Yes, he certainly had come a long way. His doctors had told him he'd come a long way.

His junior Vice—President was waiting for them at Kennedy Airport of course, just in case there might be *someone* who hadn't heard of George Killick and fail to treat him with the very special care reserved for very V.I.P.'s. Customs clearance was the slightest of formalities, and the passport control man actually came to him, seated in the deep plush of the special lounge. Nor did he have to pass through the electronic device that detected concealed weapons, but that may have been because of his Pacemaker.

The flight, in the upstairs lounge of the Jumbo which had been sealed off even to the other First Class passengers, was very smooth and uneventful; a duo of stewardesses waited on him, and once, when he fell asleep, allowed two or three others to peep in at him and wonder why a man with more than a billion dollars looked so sad.

He was not met at London, it had been his specific wish. Instead he took a cab to Claridges where he was greeted, as usual, with polite familiarity and the assurance that his usual suite had been prepared. He retired to his bed and then slept, on and off, for two days, until the inevitable weariness of the jet-lag had lifted.

On the third day, carrying only one small suitcase, he took the train to Sheffield. The scenery for the first part of the journey was very green, very British, but not too alien to George's eye because one of his many houses was situated in Maine, and another in Kentucky. It was about halfway that the industrial Midlands began to herald the North; brick chimneys, big, voluptuously waisted cooling towers magnificent under the morning sun, and then the first wheel and gantry of a coal mine, and slag heaps. Soon after that the train ran into Sheffield and George took a taxi to the Hallam Tower. A clean white modern building on the edge of the town, possibly not the best hotel, but the tallest, and George had reserved a room on the top floor, and from there he looked out across Sheffield, surprisingly small and compact from this vantage, with steep little hills ascending from every main road and somehow reminding George of San Francisco. The city was dirty, yet paradoxically the air felt and tasted clean; because it swept down from the moors. George could see those too, far away on the horizon. He had bought a map in the foyer and now pin-pointed the location of the farthest church spire he could see, he knew that beyond that, some ten miles beyond that, was his own home town.

When George got behind the wheel of the little automatic sedan the hire car people had sent over he had a moment of panic, a feeling he should go back immediately to London and fly home, but then the feeling passed and he spread his map on the seat beside him, and set off.

For the first few miles he was preoccupied with the strangeness of driving on the wrong side of the road, but then he got the knack, it became easier to him, and he began to relax and enjoy the journey. He came to a profound stop when he saw the first sign-post that pointed to his home town, and then drove on again. He knew from bitter experience that his pulse rate was up.

When George breasted the last rise he realised that he had been wrong for forty years. It wasn't big enough to be called a 'town', it was a village, no more than a village. Which is probably why it appeared to have changed hardly at all. There was a big new warehouse on the south side, and a small sprawl of some new houses, but apart from them it was exactly as George had remembered it, although albeit, some of the memories had become blurred and exaggerated. The 'King's Arms' pub for instance, where George had parked his car, he had remembered it as being much bigger, much grander, yet really it was a shabby little place. And the drinking fountain and trough for horses, which had been long defunct even in George's day, why on earth had he thought that was gilded?

But was 'The Hill' still there? George admitted it to himself for the first time that what he had really come back to see was 'The Hill'. Putting the pub at his back George crossed the road and walked up a faintly inclining road between rows of faded, terrace houses. Then a turn into a narrow alleyway, another turn at the bottom and then . . . George thought for a moment that the brick wall confronting him was new, or that he had mistaken his route, but then he remembered, and walked along the wall until he found the narrow door, and passed through, and there was 'The Hill'. In George's day it had been a grey slag heap speckled with prams and tins and other rubbish. There was still rubbish, but little grey remained to be seen, weeds and grass and wildflowers had made it their domain. The sides of the hill were very steep, but the hill itself was not that high, yet high enough for George, standing as he did now at its very foot, not to be able to quite see the top.

There was a plateau up there, George knew that, a concave dip where children could watch and giggle at the people in the village below, and yet not be seen.

George stood and stared up at the hill and heard again the thick voice of little Sammy Earnley, the pipe of Willy Comfit and the laughter of Bradshaw, Tammy Bradshaw who was so strong that he once lifted an engine block above his head. And the lilting sweet voice of Lucy Mabel.

It had been a game—not invented with the kids he played with! No, the game had tradition, it had existed as long as *anyone* in the village could remember. It had been with them all a long time. Young men feeling the first fire in their loins, but peeping shyly from behind spread fingers at coquettish, softly laughing girls who would toss their long hair and affect not have noticed. Peeping at Lucy Mabel. "You run up the hill from bottom to top, without a pause and without a stop, and there on the highest point above, you'll come face to face with your lady love." And she'd kiss you, she had to, it was part of the game, it was the tradition, and you could never break with tradition. She would kiss you and you would both vow never to look at, never to love another. For ever and ever.

The girls would go up first, walk up, swinging their skirts and turning their heads over their shoulders to look back at you, to catch your eye. Lucy Mabel's deep dark brown eyes had swept across all the fellers and settled on George, just for a moment, but he thought his heart might burst.

Once at the top they'd settle down, out of sight in the hollow, and the boys below would feign indifference. They would talk and chatter and push each other, and Bradshaw being Bradshaw smoked a cigarette. There was no official start, no 'off', a tacit agreement, the chatter would stop, and there was silence and you could hear the thump of the iron foundry on the other side of the village, and perhaps the sheep on the moors. Then suddenly they would all be running and scrambling up the hill.

George had picked his route the night before, he'd slipped out the back door and come to the hill in inky darkness, then stood for a long while until his eyes got accustomed and then made his way up the hill, picking a way that was short and direct, and trying to remember the places the slag was loose, or had crumbled to make a foot snagging pit. He was never sure, but he had thought he heard someone on the other side of the hill, someone doing the same thing.

LucyMabelLucyMabelLucyMabel, it had sung in his ears like the rhythm of a train as he sprinted up the hill, his long legs already carrying him out and beyond the other runners. The top of the hill was looming, another few strides and Lucy Mabel . . .

George blinked, the sun had gone in and the hill was a silhouette now, a dark, forbidding mass. He gripped his knee. He had been thirty-two, well on the way to his second company, before he had afforded the time and money to get it properly done, to remove the cartilage and the limp forever. Yet it still twinged on certain days.

Lucy Mabel had gone down the hill with Bradshaw, again turning her head to look at him but this time with hurt and reproof. George had sat there, holding his knee and watching her go.

He saw Lucy Mabel again after that, of course he did, but never close, and never alone. Three months later his father had taken the whole family to America. Twice, while they were in Pennsylvania, George had written to Lucy Mabel, but she had never replied, and then, while he was making his way, carving out his first million, he barely thought of her at all, and when he did it was to wonder who she had married, and was it Tammy Bradshaw? But later as he grew older and richer and idle thought was no longer a luxury he began to think of her again, constantly, and wonder.

George had never married, he'd never had the time, and when he did have the time, no longer the inclination. His friends half accepted that, but George knew it wasn't true.

The deep shadow that the hill cast over him was cold; George turned away and retraced his steps.

His own old family home looked very different. A young, recently wed couple had it now and they had painted the door bright red, a new door with panels and glass and pretentions to grandeur, there were coach lamps too, and the front garden was gone, tarmaced to provide a space for a car, the upper windows were just big squares of glass where there had once been panes, and venetian blinds behind them; the lower window had become a bay ("It would have been a bow, but we couldn't afford it")—anything to try and disguise the fact that the house was what it was, a vain effort to stand it out from the line of exactly similar dreary little houses. But the couple were nice enough and invited George in to look around and to take tea with them. George was shocked to find that the old lean-to shed in the back yard, the shed he had helped his father to build, was still there. The couple were planning to demolish it and substitute a pre-fabricated concrete hut, but they hadn't yet, and George was glad. He looked for and found his own initials cut high up into the cross beam that supported the roof, and, just an inch or two away, 'L.M'. They had sat here once upon a time Lucy Mabel and he, with a summer rain clattering down onto the roof, and talking about . . . he didn't remember what. But he did remember that that was the first time he had really looked at Lucy Mabel in THAT way. He remembered wondering desperately how a boy came to kiss a girl, how he might pluck up the courage to take those few steps across the shed and plant a kiss on the cheek of the girl he loved, because he did love her, he knew that as surely then as he did now. He loved Lucy Mabel and always did and always would.

For a moment he thought he was dreaming when he heard the rise and fall of the voice calling, "Loo-see, Loo-see," and then realised that it came from the backyard of a house further down. When the young couple told him that the 'Lucy" being summoned was 'Lucy Bradshaw', he thought his heart might stop. Then reality plunged back and he remembered that, of course, the Bradshaws had always lived there, but surely, after forty years Tammy Bradshaw would have moved on? No, the houses in this area were often occupied by generations of the same family.

American culture had reached even here, the young girl who opened the door to his knock was wearing a T-shirt and chewing gum, she looked at him with a petulant suspicion, "Lucy?" he asked and then, before she could reply, Tammy Bradshaw was beside her and glaring at him. Although Tammy had changed beyond all recognition George knew it was him, the tall body was stooped now, and the once rosy cheeks were pale and cavernous, and George recalled that the Bradshaw's had always trekked out to work down the mine, by tradition. The long years had eroded all kamaraderie so that when George explained who he was Tammy made only token noises, Tammy had forgotten everything—save the hospitality of the people in this region, without which their lot would be a very sorry one indeed. He asked George to come in, and produced a bottle of Sherry which George declined. He noticed George watching the girl who lounged against the side-board in the background, "My youngest," he said, "The only girl too, the boys are at work."

George felt himself tense, "And her mother?" he asked.

"Dead ten years ago." George sighed and sat very, still; ten years, he was ten years too late. No, he was forty years too late.

"Where is she buried?," asked George, and the question brought a frown to Tammy's face, and the girl away from the side-board, "I would like," George explained, "To pay my respects . . . "

Tammy's frown deepened, "Now why would you want to do that? You never knew Elsie, did you?"

Elsie! George was confused, "I thought, your daughter's name is Lucy, I thought you must have married Lucy Mabel."

Tammy laughed for the first and only time, "Good Lord no. She's called Lucy because, well, because Lucy isn't a bad name, is it?" and then went on, "Who's this Lucy Mabel you're talking about?" George was stunned, he couldn't possibly have forgotten Lucy Mabel, the girl who had come down off the hill with him, *his* girl!

Tammy pursed his lips, "Oh, yes, I remember her now, lived over by the stacking sheds. Lucy Mabel. Pretty little thing." His lips made a sucking sound, "She's dead too. Been dead for years." Almost forty years in fact, TB was a bad thing in those days, you would go into a decline, and a few weeks later . . . ! Tammy snapped his fingers when he explained that.

But George knew now, not only why his letters had never been answered, but that it was not just the TB that had killed Lucy Mabel. A decline yes, that was more accurate, a lack of the will to live, a pining away. He loved her more then than ever before.

11

The sun had come out again when George finally located her grave; he would never have found it if the verger hadn't been home. It was tucked between others and wildly overgrown and George had to rub lichen away with his hand to read her name. It was while he sat there quietly with Lucy Mabel that he became aware of the young girl, the other Lucy. She had followed him and now leaned on the iron gate of the churchyard, creaking it as she swung gently.

George stood up and walked towards her, and she easily fell into step with him as he walked back the way he had come, towards the hill. She was intrigued that he lived in America and wanted to know what film and pop stars he had seen and what Hollywood was really like. Way back in his balmy days George had entertained lavishly from his house in Carmel, and had actually met many famous personalities; the girl was mildly awe-struck.

The hill looked different now, the sun had moved round so that it now fell squarely on the slope and the blues and yellows of the flowers bobbed and nodded and welcomed it.

The young girl was puzzled by George's fascination with the hill, and George felt a momentary sadness, "They don't do it any more then?"

"Do what?" demanded the girl. George might have explained, but then didn't, he just stood and looked up at the top of the hill and wondered why so much of the world changed, but rarely for the better. After a while the young girl got bored and set off to go home, but just before she disappeared from sight she turned and looked at George over her shoulder, just as Lucy Mabel had done so very long ago. Then George was alone with the hill again. But he didn't feel alone, he knew Lucy Mabel was nearby, just at the top of the hill. He looked at it now, taking it in from bottom to top in a slow, sweeping glance, a glance that hesitated and held for a moment on that area just below the rim, where forty years before his running, eager foot had found and tumbled to an unsuspected hole. Then he looked at the very top; a small breeze was moving the shrub and foliage up there, tugging at it as it might tug against a mane of long brown hair. The breeze quickened and moaned ever so softly, so soft that only George heard it, like a tiny voice calling out.

There was no 'off', there never had been, just a moment of stillness, a gathering of oneself, and then George was running up the hill.

He was fourteen, a boy again, the pain stabbing at his chest and side barely felt. He pounded upwards, sliding once, almost falling once, but never stopping. He couldn't stop, you were not allowed to stop. The pain stabbed again, more insistent this time, warning, pleading. George ran on up the steep slope, up towards the rim, the horizon, towards Lucy Mabel, for surely she waited for him there, had always been waiting, and he had kept her waiting long enough. His lungs heaved and his heart screamed and just below the rim his legs almost refused him; he willed them, forced them on and, staggering now, at last, at long last he reached the top and fell, and lay there. The pain came back again now, bigger than before and, like waves before a growing storm, coming again and again, each time with greater power.

George dug his hands into the cindered ground then lifted his cheek from it and looked up and saw Lucy Mabel, she was standing there, her hands held out to him, and smiling. He knew his heart would burst, it would surely burst.

He sighed with enormous contentment, enormous happiness; George Killick had come home again.

THE HAPPY TIMES

I DIDN'T EXACTLY BUY THE LITTLE BONHEUR FOR A song, but certainly for less than a sonata. Mind you, I would have been prepared to pay more, not only because I am always needing to constantly re-stock my antique shop, but because I liked the piece. I have always liked them; charming little writing desks with a few drawers and sometimes an elegant mirror, I have always found them so pleasing to look at. Perhaps the name has something to do with it, 'bonheur du jour'; the 'happy time of the day'—when a young lady of quality might sit down at her own private little desk and write her own private little letters. This one was particularly fine and I wondered what grand home it might have come from—what bustled beauty of the day might have sat before it. There was a sort of clue just above the lock, curlicewed monogram which, after some difficulty I thought I made out to be "M de P". French? Yes, the tapering legs with their impudent little outward curve suggested French. Not terribly old, perhaps turn of the century or just a little earlier.

I liked it so much that I took it out of the shop and put it into my own bedroom. It sat there for several weeks before I found the second secret drawer. Most of these pieces have a secret drawer which, being so easy to find, makes them something of a mockery. Of course I found it right away, but then, one day, scrummaging around for the pencil that had rolled into the main compartment, I found the really secret one. Beautifully made, slim as a Vogue model and tucked away into the back panelling. It opened immediately to my accidental touch and the letters spilled out.

There were seven of them, written over the space of three years, the first in October 1885, the last in 1888. They were all in French and all written by the same man to the same woman—Matilde de Persoul. My 'M de P' was confirmed. I remember it was a fine spring afternoon when I lay down on my bed to read the letters, and almost dark when I finished—well, my French isn't that good. The letters were fascinating; they told a whole story, admittedly from the one-sided view of the writer who signed himself 'G', but it wasn't too difficult to fill in the unsaid gaps for myself. Matilde was married to a much older man—in fact she was the *Comtesse* de Persoul. Unfortunately though the old Comte was a bit remote—in the literal sense of the word because he belonged to the Societe Geographique and was always popping off somewhere to run down a river, batten a butterfly or something. Not a good thing to do when married to someone as passionate as Matilde—and judging by the way G kept panting after her in his letters, she MUST have been passionate . . . at the bottom of one letter he begged to be allowed to kiss her beautiful . . . Age had flaked away the rest of the page so I was never able to determine her beautiful what. But kiss it he obviously did because it seems that around 1885 Matilde had a son—both she and G knew it was theirs, but the old Comte didn't tumble. No, he accepted the boy as his own and then charged off up a mountain again. I could imagine the heaves of relief from G and Matilde—I mean, a situation like that would be a bit of a problem even these days wouldn't it?

They must have been quite daft about each other—and damned care-less too. You would think that 'once bitten—twice shy' but not G and M.

Here we are again—1888—and he's put her in pod again! But things were not so easy this time. It was the Comte's silly fault. It seemed that just about the moment of conception the old duffer had to be up the Amazon chasing after a rare species of parakeet. He was away eleven months. Well, you see the point? So did G and, although he made a rather good elephant—gestation joke in his letter (good considering the stress the poor chap must have been under) it was clear that he was very worried about when the Comte returned and started asking awkward questions. Like, 'swords or pistols?'

In the very last letter G seemed to have solved the problem. Or at least put up a proposition that was so self sacrificing on both sides, that you could feel the love *they* must have felt for each other.

Matilde had given pop again—but nicely, discreetly done—away in one of those remote valleys around the Loire under an assumed name and everything. So it was all still a big secret. G's proposal was devastatingly simple; he would come to some financial arrangement and marry someone whom he did not love—and possibly did not even know at that time. The mainspring of the deal would that his wife would be told of the child—but not the identity of the mother—and that it would be adopted and brought up as their own. They don't make gentlemen like that anymore. Or for that matter, ladies either.

I had no way of knowing just how it all ended—but I thought, judging from her conduct thus far, Matilde probably accepted the deal. What else COULD she have done? I hoped it had ended happily ever after, and I put the letters away—more as a confirmation as to the age of the bonheur as anything, and completely forgot all about them.

Until Benny invited me down to stay at his place in Antibes.

Benny is the dealer who confounded us all by sinking every penny of his money into Samurai swords about three minutes before the economics and the printed circuit caused us to forget about Changi and the River Kwai and welcome the first Japanese millionaire to Heathrow. Benny made a fortune, and most of it is sunk into an exclusive little shop in Nice, a huge, vulgar villa at Antibes, and a swimming-pool which, when they hold the Olympics in France, the authorities will undoubtedly borrow for the main events.

I like Benny. He's loud and fat and gregarious, but better still he is that contradiction in terms, an honest crook. Or perhaps lovable-villain might be more apt. Before leaving, as an afterthought almost, I slipped the letters into my suitcase.

You see, not many dealers are collectors. Hoarders perhaps, putting away a 'good thing' against that day when the price goes up, but not true collectors, with the love of the true collector. I suppose constantly surrounded by a surfeit of beautiful things tends to make them blasé. Some dealers remind me of dog breeders. I have never yet met a dog breeder who didn't treat dogs with apathy, and sometimes even, actual cruelty. You and I tend to pat a dog and tickle it's ears—breeders coldly

17

assess them as a lump of merchandise . . . where's the profit? Yes, they have a lot in common with us antique boys.

That's another reason I like Benny. He's different. He *does* collect. Not fine silver or Limoges, nothing he might find in his own shop, that would be too easy. No, Benny collects stories. Anything, any article that has a story connected to it and Benny's like the first greyhound out of the trap. He has a telescope inscribed 'G. Cutler', and, as Benny points out, "George Cutler was on watch when Nelson set sail that day—so through *this* scope were seen the first ships of Trafalgar." And a fine piece of porcelain delicately decorated with perfect roses, except for the last one which ends in a long, thin smear, 'De Vere the master painter was doing that when he died. So they glazed and fired it in his memory'. A man's life in one thin smear of paint. He's got items from Scott's Expedition, and a Captain's hat from The Crimea, the Russian ball still lodged in it, its wearer saved by the fact he had contemptuously stuffed his battle orders into the crown of it; and many similarly fascinating things.

That's why I took the letters along. I thought they would amuse him.

They did too. Later that balmy evening as we sat overlooking the sea and drinking the cheap but wonderful Blanc de Blanc of the region with its hint of flowers complimenting the strong sweet perfume of the bougainvilleas.

Benny's been out here a long time so, despite the crabbed, faded hand-writing, he read them very quickly, and then flicked through them again, "But there's no conclusion," he said. I shrugged, "Have to do what I did, form your own, but it's a good story, isn't it?"

"It's a terrific story, a wonderful story, but I wish I knew how it turned out." I held out my glass for more Blanc de Blanc, "That my dear Benny, we may never know."

We went out for dinner that night, Benny, me and his delectable little French wife, Eliane. We drove up to what is probably the one of the most enchanting villages in France—St. Pau—and dined in what is *certainly* the most enchanting restaurant, The Colombe D'or.

Drinks first in the dark cool bar with its polished wood and soft eroded flag-stones. Sipping chilled kir and, shoulder rubbing with sharp young men and stunning models and the usual compliment of film people—I have always been vaguely appalled by the French chic for drinking Scotch as an aperitif *before* the wine—or even that they, in this country of the grape, drink it at all. It always seems to me to be—like having the chambermaid while waiting for Venus de Milo!

Benny was quiet and thoughtful, and later when he sat 'exterior' under the gnarled vines, he said very little. Mind you, Eliane made more than enough conversation for the three of us.

"I think the adoption went through," for a moment I couldn't think what he was talking about, "It must have gone through. Damn it, what other alternative did they have." We might have pursued the topic further but at this moment a waiter came and whispered in Benny's ear, and Benny got up and walked away to the door set into the courtyard wall.

A man was standing there, and somehow it seemed to me that Benny had been expecting him. They talked very briefly, and then money changed hands, and Benny came back to the table. He was smiling now, much more out-going, "Just a little deal," he explained, then proceeded to tuck into the superb meal.

Afterwards—several Armagnacs afterwards—we strolled along the narrow, cobblestoned streets to the car, "Listen do you fancy a drive out tomorrow?" asked Benny. That seemed fine by me. "Eliane has to go into Nice, so we can drop her off and go on from there."

Which is exactly what we did, into Nice, then on from there, inland. For the first hour or so I was quite happy in the open top Aston Martin, the sun placing warm hands on my back, but then, as we ascended higher into the mountains and the air became chilly, I began to wonder.

It was as if Benny had read my thoughts, "There's a coat in the back," I raised up in my seat, the coat billowing like a sail as I pulled it on. Then looked at Benny, "Where are we going?" He grinned, "To the Chateau Persoul." I stared at him, "For God's sake" he said, "You didn't think I'd just leave it there, did you?" "And surely didn't think the de Persoul's would be extinct? A lineage like that . . . ? Bound to be some of them still around. I located them last night," he gestured ahead, "Just outside of Guillame, and that's where we're going," I knew Benny could be impetuous, but, "What on earth are you going to say to them?"

"I've already said it," Benny replied, "Called them this morning. They're expecting us," he glanced at me, "I told them we've found some old family letters. They're very interested."

"Family letters!? They're private, secret letters. They're a bombshell."

19

"They might have been," Benny conceded, "At the time maybe—but it's nearly a hundred years ago. They'll probably have a good laugh."

I wasn't sure about that. Not at all sure.

"Anyway" Benny went on, "You are just as keen to find out what really happened as I am." But I wasn't keen. I was annoyed, I felt tricked. I sulked the rest of the way.

Huge magnificent gates were in the vanguard, then a long coil of driveway, with lush terraced lawns dropping away on either side, and finally the Chateau itself. I saw right away the one portion of it was in disrepair, it had crumbled away, been evacuated and then shored up; but a long time ago—it had already conceded the losing battle to creepers and vines.

I instinctively knew that my bonheur must have come from that part of the house.

A thin butler welcomed us, took in the Aston, at a glance and then, despite our open necked shirts, gave us the treatment reserved for quality until proved otherwise. We were ushered onto a terrace at the rear of the house and told that "M'sieur le Comte" would join us shortly. Frankly I didn't mind how long he took; I've seen some dramatic views in my time, but this one was melodramatic: the ground gently sloped away a few hundred feet, and then fell very sharply, fell far into the valley below where a snake of river winked under the sun. It was made more astonishing because, as far as one could see on either side there was not another dwelling of any kind. This magnificent spectacle belonged exclusively to one house; to one family. It was almost enough to make you turn Communist.

I heard the scrape of a foot behind me and turned to see the current Comte de Persoul. He was very tall and very, very pale, as though his height had stretched his physical resources too thin. At first I thought he held the back of his hand against his side to suppress a deep, familiar pain, but then I realised that his wrist was formed that way, permanently turned inwards and fixed. I saw too that he limped slightly, and that his left shoe was built up. I guessed a legacy of the war because he was about the same age as Benny. Once he came onto the terrace the day seemed cooler.

He was impeccably polite, offering us wine and then allowing us to drink it and accept a second glass before he broached the subject, "Err . . . you spoke of some letters?" Benny nodded, pulled them from his pocket and put them on the table. The Comte looked at them for a moment, then at Benny for further explanation. "They were written to the Comtesse Matilde de Persoul."

"To my grandmother!? And you wish to ... sell them?" Benny saw now the reason for his trepidations and quickly explained how the letters came to light, and how intriguing he had found the contents (Without actually mentioning what the contents were) and how we were not blackmailers. "I see," he sat there without moving, and then we heard it.

Benny later admitted that he too thought it was an animal, a hare caught in a gin, they make that terrible, pitiful sound. But this came from somewhere in the house, from one of the upper rooms—yes, the one way above my head with its intricate lace of latticed bar work. The sound was a woman; a woman crying! But, by God what could cause her to cry like *that*?

The Comte did not appear to have heard it at all, he still sat looking at the letters, and then stretching out a finger to flick at them, and then seeing the look on our faces. "Oh," he said, "My sister."

That was no explanation. "She is ill? Recently bereaved?" I stumbled in my poor French.

"She cries," he shrugged, "She often cries."

I'll say this for Benny, he was embarrassed too. Then the crying stopped as abruptly as it began and the Comte stood up and moved across the terrace to put his face to the view, and his back to us. "The contents of the letters are intriguing."

"How intriguing?" The view got his back now. Benny hesitated, "We ... ll. Amusing. Interesting."

"Would they upset my father?" I once saw Benny in an out of town auction room pick up a vase, blow off the dust, and discover he was holding a Ming. He didn't gawp then. But he gawped now, "Your father!? He's still alive!?"

"Of course," replied the Comte, "In his ninety-fifth year and, praise God, as hale as ever. He will be here in a moment. So, you must tell me, WILL they upset him in any way?" Benny caught my eye, then, "Why don't *you* decide?" The Comte shook his head, "Naturally, belonging as they did to his mother, he would have to see them first." He looked at Benny, and saw only the villain and none of the lovable, so his gaze turned back to me, "You have read them too?"

"Yes," I confirmed, and would have left it at that, but his eyes asked for more, "Well, I . . . er . . . I er . . . Might I ask your father's Christian names?" The Comte frowned; it was an unexpected question; equally unexpected to me, I don't know why I blurted it out. "Guy" he replied, "Guy Sebastian Louis."

"Guy." Benny and I looked at each other, "We. . . ll," I started again, but Benny took the bull by the horns, "It's the story of an indiscretion, but there must have been plenty of those in this family. And your father's a man of the world isn't he?"

I didn't turn quite green. Probably more a sickly yellow. But then the Comte laughed and I knew that, miraculously, Benny had got away with it. The Comte laughed, and I felt Benny's elbow jab into my ribs, and then we were all laughing, and the sound of our laughter started to bounce back from the valley below.

The Comte choked on his laughter eventually, and then dabbed his mouth with a handkerchief held in that curiously twisted hand, "Is *that* all?" he said, "My God for a moment I thought they might prove land title or something like that."

You have to hand it to the Frog aristos. They do get their priorities right. He chuckled again, then looked beyond us. We turned too, and then we were on our feet to meet the grand old Comte. Now he was my idea of a Comte; frail, yes, but who wouldn't be after ninety-five years in this world? But ramrod straight, a mane of thick white hair, and one of those indestructible faces, filled with exquisite sadness or hardship that Van Gogh loved to paint.

I knew then how Matilde must have felt; 'G'—Guy whoever he was must have been quite a man, if his son was anything to go by.

He listened carefully, occasionally nodding his head as Benny explained about the letters. Then finally he sat back and whispered, "A secret? Yes, I always suspected . . . a secret." Benny craned—forward to catch the words, but I knew the old boy was really talking to himself. He stood up abruptly, thanked Benny for his kindness and interest, and then held out his hand for the letters. Benny held on to them. "I've got to know," he said, "I've got to know how it turned out." The old man blinked, Benny talked, talked as only Benny can talk, and a bargain was made; Benny would hand over the letters, and in return the old boy would fill in the last chapter of the story. After he had read the letters of course. Clutching them, the old Comte de Persoul retreated into the house.

His son choked into his handkerchief again, then stuck the little finger of his deformed hand up one nostril, waggled it about, looked me straight in the eyes and winked. "Help yourselves to another drink," he said. "Won't be long. Won't be long," and scuttled away, his foot dragging. Benny grinned at me, "Our betters," he said, "Too much in-breeding," he picked up the bottle and filled our glasses.

Benny drank his at a gulp and picked up the bottle again, "Won't be long," he said, "Won't be long. Then we'll know."

A big red rubber ball came bouncing around the house onto the terrace and rolled against my feet. The child who had thrown it peeped around the corner, giggled happily and instantly retreated.

I like kids. I picked up the ball, waited for the inevitable second appearance of the child, and then feinted to throw the ball back, but didn't. I thought the child might die with laughter. I played the same game several times and I each time was rewarded by the same reaction and the fleeting glimpse of a little boy. Then, patting the ball ahead of me as I went, I crept slowly towards the corner of the house. The little boy knew what was coming and pressed back out of sight giggling in anticipation.

I stopped, and patted the ball faster now, tantalisingly close to the corner of the building—a small, pudgy hand tried to intercept the ball, and then I suddenly gathered it up and, with a big "Boo" stepped around the corner and confronted the little boy face to face at last.

Then I heard Benny calling me; heard him as though from a long way away. The old Comte had emerged from the house again, still clutching the letters. He looked from me to Benny and back again. He sat down and for a moment I thought he was going, to pour himself a drink, but then he linked his fingers and just stared at them.

I like Benny but sometimes I could kick him, "Well?" he said, leaning right in over the old boy, "What is the verdict?"

"Come on Benny," I whispered, "You can see he's had a bit of a shock."

"No," the old Comte's voice was firm, very under control, because he was working hard at keeping it that way, "I made a bargain and me . . . " he faltered now, "We *Persoul's* always honour a bargain. You wanted to know, and I shall tell you."

But I didn't want him to tell me. Not anymore.

"The letters were written by Guy Misbourne. I met him only a few times and always found . . . found him . . . ," he was faltering again,

"... Very kind." He looked up at Benny helplessly. "Benny that's enough," I grabbed his arm, "Let's leave." Benny shook me off, "Leave *now*? A bargain is a bargain, isn't it?" The old man nodded, "As you say," he took a deep breath, "Obviously, I didn't know before, but he was my father. He died in 1905. Down on the river there, a boating accident. My mother died with him." It was Benny's turn to take a deep breath now; the old boy looked at him, and his eyes seemed so much duller than before, "Until now we had always thought it *was* an accident, but ... "

"A suicide pact," said Benny, "It had to be!" Kick him? I could have killed him! He wouldn't stop either, "You still haven't told us about the other child. Was it adopted or wasn't it?"

The Comte de Persoul looked out across the valley, "Oh yes. Jeannine Misbourne. A wonderful, beautiful girl, and so like my mother."

I sat down, I knew what was coming next.

"That's probably why I married her."

I knew what the old boy was thinking. The same as me. The son with the twisted body and his sister who always cried. And worst of all the little boy; the grandson, an adult trapped in the body of a Mongoloid child.

"I married my sister," he said, and let the letters fall from his hand at last.

VERY GOOD FOR THE LADIES

I LOVED THE COLONEL, AS INDEED MY FATHER HAD loved him, and his father before him, and both their father's before that. You must excuse me if I am not explaining very well, you see, although my English speaking is quite miraculous, my English writing, falling as it has into grievous misuse, is not of the very best.

What I am trying to say, in a nutshed, is that we the Ramsinghs have faithfully served the family of Pritchard for many seasons. It was in the beginning the great Border Wars, when the Colonel Pritchard then was a Major, and the Ramsingh was my great-grandfather and rose to be a proud Sergeant of the Coloured. Since then the two families have been inseparated. I think it is perhaps because both have loved Mother India—even the first Colonel Pritchard (then a Major) when certain naughty tribesmen were trying despicably to shoot him between the eyeballs and other places, and he had to waggle his malacca cane at them in a very annoyed manner, even then Major (later Colonel) Pritchard loved the beautiful country and its people—some of whom (especially those of lower caste) were not at all beautiful.

Neither Pritchards or Ramsinghs have lived in India for a long time.

Soon after the Second Great War—which was to end all wars and bring everlasting peace, and which to my mind, has only brought ever-lasting confusion—soon after that the Colonel returned to his estate in England, and my father, his wife (my mother), my sister, brother and

myself, went with him. Not for the dole! Or the free teeth or specta-
cles—oh, no, I am telling you very straight, we have always been a hard
working family not wishing nothing at all for nothing . . . we wanted
only to continue to serve Colonel Pritchard and his family that is all.
Although at the time of the departure there was no family, just Colonel
Pritchard, because, being a dedicated soldier and later a wise adminis-
trator, he had never married. It was after we had returned to England
that he met and married Mrs. Pritchard (his wife), and she was still
quite young, whereas the Colonel was in his fiftieth year, and my father
said that was a very good thing because it gave a man time to look
around him and meditate on life—and perhaps go to the bed and make
delightful jig jigs with many other ladies first. He did not say that last
part, but I am sure he thought it because he himself was betrothed at
eleven years, and married at sixteen.

We lived in great and tranquil peace and the Colonel was very kind,
building a special bungalow in the grounds of his house to put all the
Ramsinghs in, and later helping to send my brother (who is the bright
one) to medical school, and eventually, after my dear father died,
elevating me to the very high position of butler. Or, as I preferred to call
it, Chief Steward.

We had much fun, my brother, sister and I in those early days; the
big running for the dole and free teeth by less industrious members of
my country had not yet really begun. Also we were quite, quite young and
soon after the Memsahib Pritchard married Colonel Pritchard (her
husband) she presented him with Sara (his daughter), and we grew up and
played together and came to regard her as our sister, and we all loved her
very much indeed. Not quite so much I think as Colonel Pritchard who truly
regarded her as one might regard the Star of India (Or Surrey, because that
is where we lived), and he thought the sun shone out of her eyes, and else-
where.

This may have had something to do with the fact that in presenting
the Colonel with Sara, Memsahib Pritchard's presenter had many diffi-
culties, and the doctor who served her warned her that she should never
attempt to present again. I was sad for a while when I heard this, for in
my innocence I thought this meant the end of delightful jig-jigs for the
Colonel, but I later found out that this was not truly so and that
although Memsahib's presenter could no longer present, it was still
quite excellent for the other thing.

Soon the years passed and the Colonel was obviously much older than before, and the Memsahib too, although she did not show it, she remained fair and beautiful and rosey cheeked and had developed none of those saggy portions that women are inclined to develop and was altogether very beautiful. And of course Sara was beautiful too. More beautiful, not just because she was younger, but because she was at that age that the Colonel once referred to as "The Alice in Wonderland time"; the brief moment as when the butterfly pauses from its struggles to shrug off the cocoon, and remains, just looking at the harsh world without yet becoming a part of it. She doubtless knew that changes were taking place within her (my sister knew when she was nine, but we Indians mature much more quickly—which is a great and horrendous pity because we usually die a bit faster too), but she had not yet needed to come to the terms with them.

I looked at her often and loved her most fondly, but during the looking there was no stirring in my nether regions, not such as when I visited Alma, a young lady of delightful proportions whom I met at a dance and with whom I had a big misunderstanding because she asked me if I cared to 'jig-about', and I, still struggling with the wonderful language at the time, took her at her word—and learned some other words to help increase my vocabulary. I felt no desire to congress with Sara but then, as I have already stated, she was, and always would be, like a sister to me.

All might have continued in perfect harmony for ever had it not been for the untimely appearance of Geoffrey Ryder.

The Memsahib had met him one day at the tennis club and, upon finding that he had until recently been *Lieutenant* Geoffrey Ryder, serving with the Colonel's old and extremely valorous regiment, she brought him home for tiffin.

Ryder was without denying handsome, a stocky man of muscles with the square jaw that suits a pipe (although he did not smoke), and very many white teeth which he never lost the opportunity of showing with a smile, and thick, fair hair growing down to the very front of his head in what I think they call a window's peek. He spoke in the same way as the Colonel and his Memsahib, saying 'pepper' when he meant 'paper' and addressing even the very young as 'old boy'. He wore jackets with leather patches on the sleeve, even although the sleeve was not at all worn, and trousers of twill, and a cravat at his pink neck.

He had, he said, served his term in the Army, but I always suspected that this was not so, and that HIS Colonel had perhaps had to have him cashed, and that he perhaps had left the regiment under a clown. Although he had all the airs of a true gentleman, I do not think he was one really because he frequently picked his nose in front of us, the servants, and no true gentleman does that. Except possibly a Lord, and Ryder was not a Lord. My good lord no!

The Colonel greeted him very politely but I am sure he never truly liked him, and seemed especially disapproving when he referred to me as a 'wallah'. No I do not think the Colonel ever truly liked him.

However the Memsahib did very much indeed. It was she who asked him to remain for dinner that first night.

I served a superb byrani such as only my mother can make, very hot with saffron rice and lean mutton and many sambals, and also side dishes of delicately fried onion and a vindaloo. And bindi bhaji. Ryder laughed when he saw those, and winked at the Colonel and said, "Ah, bindi bhaji—veree good for the ladies, eh? EH?" and then caught the Memsahib's eye. I am telling you I was deeply shocked to hear him speak so blatant, and in the Memsahib's presence too; bindi bhaji, which is like a cross between a cucumber and a pepper, and which some call 'ladies fingers' because of their delicate shape, IS, as we all know a vegetable of renowned properties. Once someone said to me that it was an 'Afro—dizzy' or something like that, and I was quick to point out that it came not from Africa but from India, and that if it made you at all dizzy then it would be with delight— for bindi bhaji is an excellent aid to jig-jig, it puts lead into your pensive, and so I suppose that, through the enthused actions of the gentlemen, it would, ultimately be "Very good indeed for the ladies." But I would never dream of saying that in front of one.

But say it Ryder did, and later, after he had drunk many quantities of the Colonel's Hock, he said other outrageous things; once he called the Colonel an 'old dog' as he complimented him on the youth and beauty of the Memsahib (this she liked very much) and hinted that the Colonel's capacity for jig-jig must belie his advancing years. The Colonel laughed loud at this, but there was no happiness in his laughter and he avoided the Memsahib's eyes.

At the end of the evening Ryder shook the Colonel's hand and kissed the Memsahib's (she liked that too), and then when he went to get into his little sports car with no roof, he found it would not start and the Colonel said he would drive him back to his lodgings, but the Memsahib said no, the Colonel had much work to attend to in the morning and should retire early. So she drove Ryder home.

Later I secretly sat in Ryder's sports car, because I had always coveted such a car since I heard someone say that in such a car a girl's knickers would drop off with no compulsion whatsoever. I pressed this and that button, seeking the magic one that operated the knicker dropping off device, and found by mistake that which starts the car, and the engine roared into life immediately, and I sat there and wondered.

Ryder came again the next day, and the next, and then every day for a whole week, except for the Wednesday when he took the Memsahib to the races because the Colonel was too busy, and the Memsahib returned with her hair all tousled as though she had been walking in a high wind, and yet it was a very still day.

Sara had been away visiting a friend and so did not meet Ryder until the Sunday, when he came for lunch. Clearly she was blinded to the man's obvious faults, or perhaps he reminded her somewhat of the big picture of the film star which she kept pinned up above her bed, and coveted very much in a childish way. Certainly she took to Ryder immediately. He teased her a great deal, and rumpled her hair and called her 'kid'. After lunch he played tennis with her, on the court the Colonel had had built specially but now could no longer use because 'of his knee'. And before tiffin he and Sara and the Memsahib went off for a long walk, and the Colonel remained on the veranda and watched them go, and his eyes were sad.

They came back as though from a race with Sara leading and Ryder close behind, and the Memsahib running and laughing too. I thought it unseemly, even though she wore trousers (I think those unseemly too, but I do like looking at them). Ryder said it was a dead heat and picked up the giggling Sara and whirled her around, and caught the Memsahib's eye and winked—he was indeed a great winker.

Sara had resentfulness at being sent to bed before Ryder left the house, but the Colonel quietly said that HE was going to bed early too, so they both retired and left Ryder and the Memsahib alone in the drawing room. He left about two hours later.

A few days after I heard what I had never heard before, the sound of the Colonel and the Memsahib speaking in very rising voices. Being deeply concerned, and also very nosey, I crept closer to the drawing room and listened. The downshot of it was, of course, Ryder. Apparently his landlady had thrown him out of his lodgings—this having something to do with the landlady's daughter who was, by all accounts, nubile and enthusiastic and would jig-jig like there was no yesterday. Ryder was homeless and the Memsahib had suggested that they put a roof over his blonde head for a while. The Colonel resisted this most strongly, but the Memsahib carried many arguments—that it was ridiculousness since they had many rooms to spare along the corridor from Sara; that she was in the horrors because he clearly did not trust her (that hurt the Colonel for he was a man of supreme honour) but finally she produced the strongest argument of all. She cried a lot.

And of course Ryder moved in. I did not like the arrangement a very great deal because, although I served the Colonel and his Memsahib and was proud to, with Ryder it was different. He made me feel like a servant and not the brotherhood and equality that the Labouring Government had promised me in return for my voting.

Nor did he have any sense of proprietors; when serving the morning tea I would often come across him sitting, wearing only pyjamas and robe, on the end of the Memsahib's bed, and once on Sara's. In and around the bathing too, he scarcely bothered to wear anything, and once, nothing at all. Mind you, I suspect this was because Nature in her devious manner had seen fit to endow him in such a way that even a mare might have trembled, for had it been otherwise, I am sure he would have carefully worn a robe. It was unseemly, not perhaps for the Memsahib, who having enjoyed many years of jig-jig was unlikely to be unduly shocked by such a sight—also, I knew by now that the Memsahib had probably seen his endowment often, and probably enjoyed it. But there was Sara to consider too. She stood on the first—hold of life and such things should creep into her awareness gradually, by inches. Not in feet by the yard!

Ryder's wardrobe improved though. Where before he possessed only three jackets, he now had seven, and as many suits. And a gold watch. He and the Memsahib often went up to the town to look for a flat for him, and frequently came back with no flat, but many parcels . . . mostly of clothing for Ryder.

He still teased and played with Sara, and she had now taken down the big picture of the film star and had not replaced it. Once I thought, when just the Memsahib and Sara were at breakfast together, that there was a tense feeling in the wind. Such as I vaguely remember happened just before the Monsoon, when horses grew fretful in their stalls, and people scratched at each other. Or like my sister when her season was just about to commence. I wondered if this might be the case with Sara and the Memsahib, but actually it turned out to be the dress Sara was wearing. Her mother thought it a little too indecorous, and Sara actually retorted that her mother was jealous. This baffled me because clearly the dress was such that it could not possibly have ever fitted her mother. Then Ryder came into the room, and they both eagerly went towards him.

The Colonel was much quieter these days; he no longer took his usual evening stroll through the garden with Sara (She was often out speeding through the lanes in Ryder's sports car, and I worried, but then remembered that I had tried all the buttons and found no knicker dropping device)—instead he would sit and drink his Singapore Slings, but I noticed that these days there was a great deal of Singapore, and very little Sling.

It was all coming to the boil up just before Christmas. Christmas is a festival I can understand, because it celebrates the birth of someone good. The other one, Easter, which only celebrates nailing that someone good to a piece of wood seems to me to lack the true elementals of proper joy.

I liked Christmas, and was going to like this one very much indeed because Ryder had found his flat at last—bought it in fact, but where the money came from God (or more likely, the Memsahib) only knew. He packed his bags, which were much larger now because of the many clothing he had acquired, and moved out to move in.

Then, as before, I heard voices raised in angry. I had not changed, I was still nosey, and so I again drew close to watch and listen.

The Memsahib and the Colonel were alone in the Colonel's study and the card was on the tables. She was going to leave him and go and live with the awful Ryder. She confirmed now that Ryder's endowment was no surprise to her. The Colonel just stood there, very dazed. I think perhaps he had known all along that the Memsahib had been looking at Ryder's endowment, but had thought it would go away (The situation, not Ryder's endowment). He had never thought SHE would go away because, although he jig-jigged very seldom with her these days, he still loved her dearly.

I think it was about then that Sara came into the room. The voices raised in angry were very loud and she had heard much, and everything. She said her mother could not go away and leave her father, and the Memsahib said her mind was made up. But Sara said, no, the Memsahib misunderstood, the Memsahib could not go and live with Ryder because SHE, Sara was going to go and live with Ryder. It was a shocking moment. Then the Memsahib slapped Sara's face several times and said she was a silly and young and foolish little girl.

"He wants only me," said Sara, "And I am going to have his baby!"

They stood and stared at each other, Sara and the Memsahib, and they seemed to completely forget about the Colonel. I think his knee must have been hurting him much more than usual that day because he limped over to his desk, took out his Service revolver and shot both of them dead.

I rushed into the room because shooting people dead is a very worrying thing. The Colonel just looked at me, and I had never realised before just how old he had grown. I am not a preponderously brave man, but he was very frail and I suppose I could have taken the revolver from him. But I saw his intention, saw the tears in his eyes, and I quietly withdrew. Then stood outside the door and wondered if he would like one last Singapore Sling. Then I heard the shot and realised that had I dashed away and prepared it, I would have had to drink it myself. And I seldom drink, just an occasional beer.

As one might have expected from a Pritchard everything was in apple-bed order—many hungry relatives came round of course, hoping for a mention, and some of them did get a mention, but we Ramsinghs were properly provided; there was an annual for my mother, a truss for me and a truss for my sister, and another truss to make sure my brother completed his medical training.

I eventually, considering my talents, which are in the main waiting upon others in a kind and nice way, opened my own Bengali Restaurant in London. The quality of the food and my own Immaculate Conception made it a modest but lasting success. Proudly we served the best REAL Indian food in London and I grew prosperous and enjoyed many jig-jigs with many ladies, and then I married and confined my jig-jigs to my own home. Most of the time. I would often think of the Colonel and the Memsahib and Sara and those days of tranquility, and feel sad, but I never thought to see Ryder again.

It is nearly six of the years later and yet I am recognising him immediately, he is hardly changing at all, his hair is still thick and the grin with much bluster, and he is coming into my restaurant with another three who I am taking to be the husband of some fifty summers, the wife, who is much younger, and the daughter who is very young and pretty indeed. I am standing and staring and it is the old days all over again. The bad old days.

My first thinking is to order him from my establishment, provoking embarrassment for him which I would be enjoying heartily. However, something is stopping me, or perhaps it is because I am still very nosey, so instead I am going to take the order personally. He is not knowing me from a hole in the dyke, and this is not because I am now increasingly well fed and am sporting a moustache (which my wife is telling me, tickles her fanciful) but perhaps because to him I am just a wallah, and all wallahs are looking much the same, if not alike.

They are laughing a lot and I am seeing the daughter is watching the Ryder with shining eyes, and the wife is occasionally touching his wrist (and undoubtedly thinking about the joys of touching his endowment). They are ordering curries and rice and vindaloo and then he is saying what I am expecting him to be saying, "And some bindi bhaji," and catching the wife's eye and winking in the most naughty of fashions and saying, "Veree good for the ladies, eh?" And he is chuckling deeply, but I am seeing that the husband is far from chuckling and can only indulge in the frowning.

I am serving them a wonderful meal, and then hovering not too far away to listen. And it seems that Ryder is taking the flat not so very far away, and is very anxious for the husband to be putting money into one of his schemes—which I am having no doubt is totally nefarious, if not down—up dishonest. The wife however is very keen and probably thinking even more of Ryder's endowment. And Ryder is then offering to drop certain papers in for the husband to see, but the husband is saying he will be away, and Ryder is winking at the wife and saying that he will drop them by anyway and I am seeing through him like a pain in the widow. It is when Ryder is ordering the second portion of bindi bhaji that I am getting the first glimmerings of my idea, and I am immediately dashing off to telephone my brother. And my brother, who is the doctor now, and the most ethical of men, is still remembering clearly the Pritchards and loving their memories very much indeed, and so is in the immediate agreement with me.

So I am now hurrying back and relieved to finding Ryder still there, and I am now flattering him with great outrage and telling him that from the way he is ordering I am perceiving how great is his knowledge of the Indian food, and how it is a privilegement and a pleasure to have such a man in my humble restaurant.

I am also telling him that it would make me happy beyond all recall if, the next time he is coming to honour me, he phones first so that I am able to prepare special delicacies for his tongue. Ryder's ego is liking all this very much indeed, and it is not doing him so much harm with the ladies either. And when he leaves I am knowing that I will see him again.

Later that night my brother is coming and he is bringing his bag with him.

My brother is studying well and wisely, and is now carrying many letters after his name. But he is soon perceiving that letters after his name are not enough and he is soon becoming the specialist, which is putting not more letters after his name . . . but figures into his bank balance.

He is specialising in the business of plastic surgery, and this is where ladies have their noses altered to other noses, and saggy portions of their anatomy suitably dealt with. Even men are going in for this strange thing, and my brother is telling me often of vain men who are having wrinkles replaced with smooth, and noses shortened. This last is vexing my mind terribly because I am knowing that the size of a man's nose is telling much about the size of his endowment and that to tamper with such things is, to my mind, most fooling hardy.

Many times in the past my brother is telling me these things and I am laughing like the drain. Then he is becoming more serious and explaining that some of the things he does is not for vain but for well meaning purposes. He is telling me then about men who are born with very tiny endowments, so that really they are girls under all; and girls who are born with huge endowments (where girls usually have the tiniest and most delectable ones, and decorously tucked away too), and my brother is snipping off the one, and sticking on the other and the boy who was really the girl is now looking like the girl and vice versa, and everyone is very happy but personally I am finding it altogether very confusing and also because I am very nosey (but would never think to have it shortened) I am asking questions of my brother about whether it really works, and afterwards can they ever have the proper jig-jigs such as I am enjoying with my wife (and others on occasions when she is away or not looking). It is then that my brother is explaining and I am getting the perfect idea. It seems that in addition to the snipping off and the sticking on there are many wonderful and various Hormones—this is spelt quite correctly because I have the package right before me and am also seeing the words, "To be administered under medical care only."

These Hormones are to be treated with the uppermost care because they are having the most hilarious effects, acting as they do on those parts situated beneath a man's endowment—and in other more mysterious places in ladies. They are changing, as my brother is most carefully explaining, 'the characteristics' and this proverbially is meaning that which is making the man the jig-jigger, and the woman the one who is jig-jigged. These wonderous Hormones are sometimes being given by the needle and sometimes by the mouth, but obviously, in Ryder's case we are using the mouth . . .

It is all but over now, and so I can write in a less hurried manner, not that I mind writing, finding that, since I became of a rounder and more manly shape, it is one of the few occupations that does not bring the puff to my chest.

Ryder has been a tedious regular customer in my restaurant for many months now, and this is certainly explicable because I am pretending to be his friend of the bosom, and never accept his money at all now. He eats a great deal, and always huge portions of the bindi bhaji, and that is where my brother and I are putting most of the Hormones.

In the beginning we noticed no changes at all, and in the beginning he was always bringing many and various ladies in to dine with him-sometimes the wife I saw him with previous, and some other times new and other ladies and there was always much laughing and giggling and the touching of knees and other places.

But of late he has been dining here alone, and the changes are now of some notice; his voice is no longer deep as before but is becoming shrill like the screech of a parakeet—in particular when he laughs, but he does not laugh nearly so often these days.

His lips seem to have grown more full too, and lush like a ripe plum, and his skin, which was always very fair and English is now like the peach blooming—in particular on his face where there is no longer beard, but a sort of down such as one finds around the more delicate regions of a duck. Also, it may be my imaginings, but his nose seems to be getting smaller.

I think though, that in a few days time I am going to be telling him that he is no longer welcome here. It is because the front of his chest is now so full and rounded that he can no longer hide it, and other customers are beginning to point and whisper and set him blushing girl-ishly, and wonder just what kind of a place I am running here.

Anyway, I have two sons of tender age, and I cannot afford to take any chances.

WALT

WALT WAS THE REINCARNATION OF W.C. FIELDS; he was fat, red faced, blue nosed and he boozed and he swore and most of all he hated kids.

He almost hated me when I joined him, but I was nearly eighteen then and didn't really qualify, so he didn't actually hate me, but he didn't like me either. Mind you, he didn't *like* anyone, but he actively hated kids. If he saw school kids crossing a road he'd speed up. He'd pop their balloons with the end of his cigar, tread their toys underfoot and once got a real kick when he watched one of them nearly drown off Malibu, "But one of those life-guards came along and *interfered*," he scowled.

I often wondered if his hatred was a result of some deep seated incident way back, or maybe a series of incidents because in the early Thirties when Walt started in the business, there were a lot of child stars in the movies. And that's where Walt and me worked, in the movies.

My dad was a cameraman but even in those days a union ticket was hard to come by, and you had to take what you could get, so I started with Walt; in special effects. I suppose because Walt disliked everyone else so much they retaliated and didn't like him either, but there was nobody in the industry who wouldn't admit that Walt was the best special effects man there was, perhaps ever would be.

It was funny really but, with my dad in the business, and the house always filled with technicians and writers, and sometimes a star or two, I didn't really know that much about special effects; I thought it was a matter of pulling down walls with ropes, and blowing up bridges and things without actually removing any part of the actor's anatomy. Walt soon taught me there was more to it than that, and he was a good teacher too because his work was about the only thing he ever really loved; I learnt to listen, and not talk too much, and never, NEVER interrupt, and it was fascinating. We fixed lines to make horses fall, and dug pits for them to fall gently into because Walt didn't hate horses, and created fires that would spread to within three feet of the camera and not an inch more. We derailed trains, and laid artillery fire, and blew make believe arms and legs off and even one decapitation; we made elephants fly, and men invisible and whole cities fall down before your very eyes, and pixie villages spring up, and pretty soon I'd forgotten my ambition to follow my dad and become a cameraman. Then around the Fifties I was glad I hadn't; television had brought the big movie slump then, and even my dad was out of work, but Walt and me, we never stopped, because he was the very best and I was his assistant. By now of course I was handling a lot of the rigging of the more standard work myself, and once he let me do almost a whole picture on my own, but that was a Disney movie, and had a lot of kids in it.

I think that, apart from his meticulous attention to detail, what set Walt way up above the rest was his lack of resistance to change, to anything new. Our industry is full of old guys who sit around talking about "They don't make them like they used to," and when they do make them as they used to, wondering why nobody goes to see them. Not Walt, he knew before anyone that audiences were getting more sophisticated, and television was partly to blame—Hell! You could see a dozen cars crashed every night—but weak stuff, a simple bump against a tree or even cheating and having it happen off screen. Walt knew that pretty soon the audience would want, would *demand* to see the car disintegrate in full view, and then maybe a lot of cars together, and see too what happened to the drivers, and lots of blood. Even the days of miniature models were slipping away, "Goddammit!" Walt once said, "If we get a script where the White House blows up, that's what we're gonna have to do! They won't accept anything else." I didn't say anything, but I thought at that particular time blowing up the White House while occupied might not be such a bad thing at that!

We flirted with television occasionally but it wasn't really for Walt; they were cheapskates some of them, and there were too many grey suited executives who cared a lot about ratings and money, and nothing about movie making—generally because they didn't have the faintest idea about it.

So one day after they sent Walt his Academy Award (He had four and never once went to collect) for his work on a big science fiction picture, the company that made it came round to do a deal. They had a big programme ahead of special effects pictures and they wanted Walt for a five year exclusive contract. It was academic to me because naturally I would go where Walt went.

He settled for it, in the main because it gave him a big budget to play and experiment with, but also because it flattered his ego, he would have his own workshop, trailer on site and on some of the movies would be as important as the director. It would also make him a very rich man indeed.

It was soon after that that I came across Walt working late one night in the big, new, lavishly equipped workshop; he had a calculator taken apart, not one of those little pocket things, but a big desk model that was as near as damn it a real computer. Walt was studying the circuits and touching this and that one with his screw-driver; I momentarily wondered how he had managed it with HIS shaking hands, but then he turned and grinned at me and I knew he was sober. He was sober occasionally, when he was working on something really important. "Electronics," he said, "They're here to stay, and we've got to get with them, boy." He still called me 'boy' although I was nearly forty now and my eldest son was sixteen. I had three kids and maybe Walt knew about them, but he never mentioned them, and neither did I. Sometimes I had thought I would, sometimes I thought Walt had mellowed with the years because only rarely now did he stand by the commissary window and throw stones at the school across the way, though it is true that once, not so very long ago, he HAD crept out at night with a sledge hammer and smashed up the children's play park the city had built at the end of his block, but he had been very drunk at the time.

For the next few weeks I was in Thailand working out the way to shake an ancient temple as though in an earthquake, and then have it explode from within. It was a simple enough job, but took time to rig.

When I got back I knew Walt had finished whatever he had been working on because even if he had wanted to stand up and shake my hand (and he would never have wanted to, not in a million years)—he couldn't. He just lay back on his filthy bed and cradled the Bourbon and grinned at me in a lop-sided way.

The whole house was filthy and always had been. Walt had never married and, although I would never have dared remind him of it, he had once told me why. "It's women" he had growled, "Bring a woman into your life and you know what you're going to do, don't you?—And once you start doing that you know what's going to happen? Kids. *Babies!*" and the horror in his face as he said that had to be seen to be believed.

I sat gingerly on the edge of the bed and waited while he took another long pull at the bottle, and then waved a vague hand and said, "Over there . . . cupboard . . . in a box."

I opened the cupboard, took out a closed cardboard box and brought it back to the bed, "Go ahead" he grinned, "Open it" I did, and I saw what I first took to be a ventriloquist's doll, certainly it was about the same size, and all hunched up in the box. As I took it out it hung lax in my hands, "Put it down" said Walt, "Down on the floor," and from under his pillow took a little panel with buttons and lights and switches. The doll lay where I put it, like a pathetic little heap of rags, Walt grinned, "Watch," he said, and pushed a button.

One of the most difficult pictures for a special effects man is the monster picture; usually you have to build several models of the same monster, one is larger than life (all monsters, by definition, are always larger than life, sometimes than the Empire State), then there are other scaled down versions, and finally quite small ones, made of clay or rubber or plastic material. The trick is to make them move, and the way that is done is that you take the monster's limb, move it just a fraction, photograph it, move it again a fraction, photograph, and so on, until you have hundreds, maybe thousands of photographs, and you put them together and run them like one of those flick-picture books, and . . . the monster raises its arm. It takes a lot of time and patience, and more important, a lot of money. The end result isn't that perfect either, there is often a jerkiness that betrays the illusion.

Walt's little doll sat up, opened its eyes, and then Walt pushed another button and it stood up, quite naturally as you or I might!

It ran, it danced, it took a cigarette in its tiny hand and affected to light it, and finally it came over and took my hand and I just sat there astonished

Walt pushed himself up off his bed and came across and lifted the doll high into the air and inspected it for a moment with, his bleary eyes, then suddenly brought it crashing down against the side table shattering its head from its body and scattering the room with tiny electronic components. "I made it too small" he spat, "It looks like a damned kid!" Except he didn't say 'damned'.

It didn't matter of course, Walt carried the blue-print in his head and, whatever reason he gave, it *was* too small for our purposes; the next film in the schedule was a monster ape from outer space and Walt confounded all previous practice by building only one model of the thing, life size as scripted. We built the thing together, and they had to put up special scaffolding for us to work from. When it was finished it stood just over thirty two feet high, and its giant hands spanned four feet across. It was sensational!

There was debate as to whether it should be kept a secret or not, but finally the publicity boys agreed that the pre-publicity of such a marvel could only stimulate interest in the finished picture and so we held an unveiling. Literally an unveiling, and a team from wardrobe burned midnight oil sewing silk squares together to cover the beast.

Pressmen have got used to everything being 'the biggest' and 'the greatest' so when they entered the stage that had been cleared specially, and saw the silk covered mound, they weren't too impressed, but then Walt started to press buttons and they saw the silk covering start to move from within and there was a ripple of comment. The silk bundle stood up and grew taller, and then fell away and the great ape was revealed. One of the girls screamed, but mostly they were awed, then thrilled and excited as Walt put it through its paces.

It came forward and the ground trembled, then they were all laughing as it pirouetted, extending its arms in a grotesque parody of a ballet dancer. Flashbulbs were popping now and it coyly hid its face and peeped at us from behind one huge hand, then suddenly reached out and encircled the prettiest of the female reporters with its fingers, and picked her up, and extended her, kicking and giggling hysterically, high,

high above its head. And then gently put her to the ground again. They were applauding now, and the studio executives were preening themselves. It turned its attention to the studio manager, a taciturn man who was always rousting Walt about over—spending, and, to his alarm, it now picked him up, and those thick fingers began to tighten, and the man became very red in the face. I glanced at Walt and saw that the drink was getting to him now, and there was a look in his eye I didn't like, so I gently took the control panel from him, then urged him away towards the tables set out with cocktails, and put the man down again.

It made all the wire services and the front page of practically every paper in the country; two rival companies planning monster pictures of their own 'temporarily' abandoned them, and City money which had been tardy until then now came pouring in. We were a hit before we had rolled an inch of film!

Drunk and irascible or not Walt was clever, he had kept a loophole in his contract so that the monster, and the idea behind it, remained his property and the studio could only lease it from him. That loophole might really have been the beginning of things between him and Cole.

The head of the production, the man who had originally contracted Walt, died suddenly (but happily, judging by the mink his favourite starlet wore at the funeral) and the board working on the theory that anyone who had been content to work under him was, and always would be, just an underling, brought in a new man from outside. They brought in Cole.

Cole was of the new school. In the old days production chiefs did practice nepotism to an enormous degree, standing like emperors over all they surveyed— which invariably included some of the dishiest, sexiest girls in the world, swimming pools, booze and wild parties that didn't often get into the papers if they were very careful and spread their money wisely. Cole wasn't like that, he knew that these days even ACTORS could run for Governor, and also, like most Californians was determined to live forever. Not that he was that old, in fact he was younger than me and what's more if he had been older would still have looked younger than me, because he was your push-ups and clean-air and honour-thy-body man. I don't think Cole cultivated his image, I think he was honestly born that way. He should have been a priest really.

He had a wonderful house on Mandeville, and a wonderfully beautiful wife whom some said was STILL a virgin, even though she had given Cole three wonderful sons. Yes, Cole had kids. What's more, perhaps this time *consciously* veneering his already immaculate image, he liked kids. He ran trusts for them, sat on the boards of orphanages, organised outings; if he did have his eye, one day, on the Presidency, he would ride in on the kiddy vote. On a skate board.

Cole, of course, inherited the monster picture. And Walt.

The writers and director felt his influence first when changes were ordered, changes not always for the better, but backed up with a, "Would you like YOUR children to see this?" It became a catch phrase around the studio, and our giant ape grew more loveable every minute. He didn't tear things down anymore, he resurrected them.

Walt must have known it was Cole, it's true they had never actually met, but he must have known—after all, Cole was his boss. Nevertheless when Cole entered the workshop for the first time, Walt took one look at him, and at the six year old boy who held his hand and said . . . well . . . what you would expect Walt to say under those circumstances. A mild translation would be, "Please go away—now." I was there and I thought Cole was going to burst, it was not just the insolence, but THOSE words, in front of the child.

He was going to fire Walt right off, but the money men who had put Cole in now pointed out three things, that they would be breaking Walt's contract and it would cost a fortune; they wanted Walt's monster; and finally if it came right down to a 'him or me', it would have to be Cole.

Cole was sharper than Walt, or so I thought at the time; he started a war of attrition. It began with the script changes, before there had been just a couple of teenagers for the Great Youth of America to identify with, but now kids crept in. Not just one or two, but legions of them, in every scene practically. Walt would have to work alongside kids all day. Increasingly, after we started shooting the picture, he gave more and more over to me, and I became very expert in controlling his marvellous ape. Walt would retire to the workshop or his trailer, and close the blinds on the many kids wandering around the lot, and drink. Cole went one better however, he had been through that contract of Walt's with a toothcomb, and discovered that he had to 'comply with studio practice'. Studio practice became an endless stream of 'open days', visitors from outside, and Cole with his special interest in various childrens' societies made quite sure that every contingent contained a majority amount of kids. It was part of the tour to see every aspect of film making, and that included Walt's workshop. He took it for about three days, and then retreated into his trailer. Cole then brought in his family plan; quite a number of the studio staff and actors et al were divorcees or one parent families, or their wives went out to work, and Cole catered for them. He set aside a building as a school and nursery where such parents could bring their children while they worked. He even set up a special playground for them. It was quite a popular scheme, except with Walt because the playground was right outside his trailer!

So Walt started working from home, but Cole pursued him even there. As a prominent civic member with children's welfare especially at heart, he began to lobby for permission to turn Walt's block into a play street.

That was what finally broke Old Walt; he had lived in the house for nearly thirty years and was too old and too tired to move.

They had a brief and private meeting, I saw Walt go off to it and I saw him come back to collect his things, he was sober, but looked sad and very weary. Defeated it seemed. They had struck a deal, Cole would call off the play-street and in return Walt would let them buy him out of his contract, but he also had to sign over his monster. Walt wasn't going to be very rich anymore.

I asked him what he would do now. "I dunno," he said, "Sit and think," I tried visiting him a few times after that, but he rarely answered the door and when he did he was stoned out of his mind most of the time. Then we got to the really tricky scenes in the picture and I got very busy and didn't see him for two months or more. I thought about him a lot though, his training stood me well, the studio was pleased, and already there was talk of maybe an Academy for me this year, or at least a nomination.

The picture was cut and finished and released; it made two million in the first week and was well on its way to being the block-buster of all time. We were already carefully building *two* new apes for the sequel, even more refined than Walt's original which had been consigned to the scene dock.

I called Walt a few times and he sounded brighter now, but still declined my offer of dinner—I even risked asking him home because my youngest was nearly fourteen now and what the Hell!

My relationship with Cole was professional but pretty cool, no matter what the provocation I still didn't like what he had done to Old Walt, so it came as something as a surprise when he asked me the favour. He said at the time it would help promote the sequel, but I knew he was really only promoting himself. Nevertheless I agreed, and it was announced in the papers and caused quite a bit of excitement.

Two days later Walt turned up; I was working late over some circuitry and he had never actually been banned off the lot and suddenly he was there, grinning at me just as it had always been.

I hesitated before I offered him a drink, but surprisingly he said no, "Not until I've got something to celebrate," and then we just sat chatting about the old days, and my Academy nomination (He made light of that, but I knew that secretly he was proud of me) and this and that. Then finally he said, "How is the old feller?" For a moment I couldn't think what he meant, but then I realised he was talking about the ape, HIS ape. The ape Cole had taken from him, I had never known Walt be sentimental before, but he sounded sentimental now so that when he asked me if he "Could see the old boy, just one more time?," I agreed, and got the key to the scene dock and took him there.

It had gathered some dust, and here and there the ape skin had taken a beating, but it still looked impressive. Walt stood and looked at it and I was reminded of man and his monument.

I was terribly, desperately embarrassed when Walt began to cry, I didn't know what to say or do for a moment, and then I put an arm around his shoulder, and that's when he collapsed. He lay there gasping, "Pills," he said. "Pills . . . my car." I turned and ran, way across the empty studio to the parking lot, but that too was empty. He must have parked it outside. I ran through the gates, shouting at the solitary gate-keeper if he had seen Walt's car.

It was parked right down at the end of the block and when I got to it and opened the glove compartment It was full of grubby, thumbed books so that I had to search it twice before I finally found the tiny, anonymous pill box.

When I got back he was still lying where I had left him, but his breathing was easier now, and certainly, after he had swallowed two of the little white pills he seemed to recover quite quickly.

I helped him to his feet, and would have taken him back to the workshop, or driven him home, but he insisted that I just take him back to his car and he would be all right. Before we left the scene dock, he paused for a moment, and threw up a half mocking salute to the ape.

I called him later that night and he made light of the incident, then I called him the next morning and he sounded not cheerful —Walt was never cheerful—but more his own self, I promised I'd drop by and see him that evening, and then I was busy supervising the loading and the transport, and finally, at the venue itself, setting the whole thing up.

Cole arrived early and insisted that we keep it covered up, "For effect"; I tried to argue with him that we should have a trial run first, but he wouldn't hear of it. Anyway he was right, there really wasn't time because already the park was filling up.

The sound of ten thousand children is curious, like the constant twittering of many birds, vaguely irritating, and I almost, ALMOST, understood Walt's point of view.

They were Cole's children, from the homes and orphanages that he endorsed, and his PR man had made sure that every newspaper knew they were Cole's children. We were to be the main event, me and Walt's ape, and at exactly twelve noon I unveiled him and a loud gush of delight floated across the open ground.

Cole smiled at the carefully selected dignitaries nearby, then nodded to me. I pushed the button of the panel and the ape began to move, to stand up; I thought I would take him to the edge of the stage apron first, then let him teeter with that marvellous off balance trick that had so delighted the movie goers, then turn him around in his equally delightful pirouette.

I pushed the button again. And the ape stepped down off the stage.

I remembered Walt then—crying. And Walt had never cried in his whole life. He was incapable of tears. The pills! Asprin? And the heart attack a fake. Most of all though I remembered those books in the glove compartment, grubby, well thumbed books; Advanced Electronics. Remote Control. *Pre-Programming.*

I pushed another button then, then another, then all of them in the hope of fusing it. Cole glanced at me with a frown, his face wasn't pale yet. Not yet. And the ape continued its relentless advance towards the kids, thousands of kids. All screaming now. In anticipation.

THE POWER OF THE PRESS

SOME 300 KILOMETRES NORTH OF NAPLES THERE IS a village, and just close by a wood nestles against the side of a hill, and in the middle of the wood is a Lamborghini. It has this year's registration, less than 2000 kilometres on the clock. Yet already sweet columbine is growing through the dash and squirrels are nesting in it.

Since none of the villagers (save for Old Georgio) could read or write, not even a postman came to the village. Except just twice, during The War, and then only to inform them that the two young men summoned from the village had been killed. No one regretted not seeing a postman anymore. It is true that once upon a time, a Sergeant from the police post way below in the valley used to call. He would sit and perhaps drink half a bottle of wine and pass the time of day, and then go and pay his respects to the widow of his old friend. Sometimes it would be way, way after dark before he had finished paying his respects to her, but then both he and she grew older; and she very fat indeed, and neither the widow or the village had seen the Sergeant in—what?—eight years. Even Old Georgio could not remember exactly, and he had become calendar, historian, and general mentor to the village as the years had passed.

So the sight of a man riding a moped up the curving, dusty path towards the village had been an occasion for great excitement.

Luca had seen him first, from his perch high up where the thin tumble of stream began, and where he minded his father's small herd of goats.

He stood up, shielded his eyes and listened to the faint 'put-put' of the small motor for some moments, and then went running, jumping like a goat himself to warn the villagers that a stranger was on his way!

Luca's father, who tended to treat his son with equal measures of severity and contempt, was so excited that he even forgot to order the boy back to attend the herd. Luca thought it felt like Christmas. The widow rushed home to put on her best frock with the red flower on it, and Old Georgio, perhaps remembering those two visits the postman had made many years before, crossed himself and again silently promised that he WOULD make the trip across the valley to the nearest and only church. One day.

The stranger was a grave disappointment, and they all spoke of it every day for many weeks afterwards. A thin, irritable man with a city accent, who declined their eager smiles and hospitality, and even worse—their wine; and who was dressed, as Franco succinctly put it, "As though he were always ready to be invited to a funeral." It turned out that he had something to do with 'Census', and Old Georgio later confirmed with great authority that this was a religious movement. A great many candles burned before a great many ikons that night.

Apart from this renewal of Christian fervour, the stranger left them another legacy, the newspaper. Not knowing right away that the stranger intended corrupting their beliefs, Luca's father had proudly offered him the benefit of his privy, which, in its day, with its *porcelain* bowl (Leading down, as did everyone else's, onto the good earth below) had been something of a status symbol. It was in that privy that Luca found the newspaper—some of it, understandably, torn away—but he only got the merest glimpse of it before his father snatched it from him and beat him about the head with a stick, driving him away up the hill and back to his goats again.

At first Luca's father was tempted to burn the newspaper. Like the rest of the villagers, he had not seen a paper in a long, long time, and his first glance at it had sent his hand creeping up to touch the olive wood cross he always wore at his neck. Some of the women depicted in the photographs! One . . . well . . . she was showing parts of her body that even his wife—God rest her soul—had never allowed him to see. Yes, he really ought to burn it. He kept the paper for three weeks before he eventually showed it to Old Georgio.

Meanwhile Luca sat on his hill with his goats and wondered about his father's lack of respect for him; after all, not only was he the eldest child, but also the only son, and yet his father treated him like a fool. His two sisters on the other hand . . . his father never beat them over the head with a stick, and sometimes even laughed and joked with them.

Luca was glad he had seen the newspaper if only briefly, because at last it had solved for him the mystery of the bumps both his sisters had on their chests. Indeed all the women in the village had them and Luca had a deep suspicion that *they* were the reason his father favoured his sisters before him. He knew that his father secretly coveted such bumps, and especially those of Signora Garrini, who's bumps were very, very large indeed. Yet Luca had now seen such bumps naked in the newspaper and still could not understand what all the fuss was about; they were not *ugly*, that he would admit—on the other hand they merely reminded him of a cake someone had once given him at Festival time; the cake itself had been dry and tasteless, but the cherry on top had been delicious.

When Old Georgio saw the newspaper he was more sanguine about the pictures of the women. Nevertheless, he held onto the paper for two weeks before it eventually became communal property.

One sultry evening Old Georgio produced the paper for all to see— although, of course, out of deference to the women of the village, he had carefully cut out the offensive pictures and destroyed them. Or at least he said he had, Luca's father was never totally convinced of that. The now inoffensive paper passed from hand to hand, and many heads nodded wisely over the incomprehensible newsprint and clucked over the photographs of automobiles and strange machines (which Old Georgio assured them were for washing things and keeping things cold) and the many faces of anonymous men and women.

Luca especially enjoyed this time; savouring a sense of secret power— HE knew what the holes in the paper had once contained.

By a unanimous vote it was the front page of the newspaper that everyone liked most. This bore a headline that *everyone* could under-stand: "20,000,000 Lira!" They would say it aloud, "Twenty million lira" over and over, and smile, and heads would shake, and elbows would nudge ribs. Just looking at it made them feel good. It made Luca laugh out loud, because he knew it was obviously a joke—twenty million lira!?—everyone knew that there never had been, could never possibly be, so much money in the world.

Old Georgio saved that story until last. Over the space of ten days—and even the wine making was neglected for it—Old Georgio would squat down, take up a page of the newspaper, and read aloud a story.

Luca loved it. Even the stories which were about people and places he had never heard of and he didn't understand...he loved every minute. Unfortunately some of the stories were never completed. Luca's father blamed the stranger for that, and everyone agreed with him; any man who refused their wine—wine renowned for its settling, therapeutic affect—well, he DESERVED to, have used a lot of paper in the privy!

On the penultimate evening Old Georgio turned to the front page, and the insuck of many mouths made a little sigh on the air. Then Old Georgio slowly folded the paper and nobody questioned him. They knew that *tomorrow* night he would read *that* story to them.

Luca did not sleep at all that night. He sat on his hill and prodded at his goats in a desultory manner, and thought. Twenty million lira! What could the story be about? Who were the grim faced men in the photographs? And the pale young man, being embraced by the older woman who looked as though she MIGHT be his mother? And his head all swathed in bandages?

The next evening Luca was first in to the square. Taking up a position beside the rim of the crumbling wall Old Georgio always sat on.

The widow kept them waiting. Luca could have killed her for it. Killed her! Then, panting, and pulling a shawl around her shoulders she entered the ring of villagers, planted her ample behind into the dust and Old Georgio unfolded the newspaper at the front page, and began to read.

Later, at least two months later, controversy still raged throughout the village. Some said that Old Georgio, capitalising on their ignorance, had exaggerated outrageously, others—those few who had at sometime made at least one visit to the town in the valley below—said not that it WAS true. But that it COULD be true.

Luca believed every word. Except for the actual money of course, that had been Old Georgio's embroidery, but the substance of the story; Luca believed it utterly.

Eventually, with the news being fairly allocated (for strictly controlled periods) to every household in the village, it began to disintegrate, and finally (again in strictly controlled portions) ended up where it had begun, in a privy. Or rather many privies, scattered across the village. The story passed into legend but, with a particularly severe winter and Signora Garrini giving birth to twins, it lost its immediacy, its impact. Yet still some evenings, when there was a lull in conversation, Luca's father might suddenly grin and say, "Twenty million lira, I'd give my right arm for that!" and the men would chuckle along with him.

Luca loved such moments because, although he never understood the mysterious joke, it meant that, for a short while the story might be revived and discussed again. Once he had even dared to make the remark himself, "I'd give my right arm," but the men hadn't laughed on that occasion. Instead, his father had cuffed him around the head and said that "Even twenty million lira would not buy you any brains." Luca never attempted to introduce the story into the conversation again, but he never forgot it. Most days he would sit on the hill with his goats, his mind trying to come to terms with the enormity of it. On this particular day however, he was not on the hill.

"The Road" was not a place Luca went to often. Once upon a time, when just a small boy, he had taken a stick and the old iron hoop from the wheel of his father's broken cart, and sent it scuttling along "The Road." That had been when the road was comparatively new, with clear tarmac, and a hoop might roll unimpeded for as far as a little boy could run.

Since then grass had sprouted up between the cracks, and then long sharp nettles, and latterly smell shrubs, so that now, one had to push aside thick foliage to find that there had once even been a road.

It was however a wonderful place to sharpen a knife.

Many years before there had been talk of a big, foreign factory coming into the area and an eager authority had started the road, but the factory went elsewhere, and the road was abandoned so that it now ran up from the valley and abruptly stopped. A forgotten road, going nowhere.

Once the end of the road had been littered with discarded building materials, but gradually the villagers had filched everything they could move, so that now there were just four large granite blocks remaining. One of them had acquired a curved scar that exactly matched the sharp blade of Luca's knife.

For just a brief moment Luca thought, the sound was approaching thunder, but then he scrambled up on top of the granite block, gazed down the road, and saw the car. A slash of red and glitter travelling very fast, sheer power scything it through, but starting to skid now, to veer from side to side as the undergrowth beneath its low slung body began to build up, and eventually halt it. Luca thrust his knife into his waist-band and started off down the road.

They were both out of the car; the girl was tall and thin, much thinner than any woman Luca had ever seen before. His father would have given her barely a glance; her bumps were very small indeed. There was something about the young man that reminded Luca of that other young man, the one with his head swathed in bandages on the front of the newspaper. They were shouting angrily at each other, "You fool," yelled the girl, "You ... " she used a short word that Luca had never heard before. The young man suddenly laughed, and drew deeply on his cigarette, the way Old Georgio did when tobacco was low and he wished to savour every fragment. His laughter too, reminded Luca of Old Georgio, when he had been drinking too much wine.

"Haven't you always wanted to do something like that?" said the young man, "Haven't you always?"

The girl wasn't laughing, "You are high," she said; a remark Luca never understood because the young man wasn't that tall, "You're high, and you are damned dangerous."

"And you" retorted the young man, "Are a ... " Now *he* used the short word that Luca had never heard before. The girl made claws out of her hands and advanced on the young man, "You have ruined the car," she said, "You have ruined my birthday present." The young man now took her hands and held her there, "Well, your daddy will buy you another one, won't he? Your fat, rich ... (That short word again) ... of a daddy?" This seemed to bring out a strength in the girl that Luca found surprising in one so thin, and with such little bumps.

She screamed, pulled her hands free and scratched at the young man's face, and he in turn began to slap at her. For a moment Luca was lost, remembering the days when his mother had been alive.

Then, astonishingly, they stopped fighting and the young man held the girl close and kissed her. She struggled for a moment, then relaxed against him. Then she pulled free, "No," she said, and her voice was much softer than before.

"Why not?" the young man asked, and looked around him; but Luca, who had often stalked and caught rabbits with his bare hands, was deeply hidden. "Come on" said the young man and flicked his cigarette away, "This is the day for madness." He kissed the girl again, and this time she laughed, "All right," she said, "But I insist on being comfortable," and she moved to the car, pulled out a woollen rug, then stood for a moment, looking at the thick nettles. The young man took her hand, "Down the slope" he said, "There's grass down there." Together they climbed over the rim of the road and disappeared down the hill beyond.

Luca padded forward on his rabbit stalking feet, found the still smouldering cigarette end and carefully ground it under his heel. City people! They did not understand about the brush fires that could leave a village poor for a whole year or more. City people! He stood looking at the car. Although Luca had seen no more than a dozen cars in his whole life he knew that *this* car was the property of someone very rich, and had he not heard the young man confirm that the girl's father was rich? "Rich," that was very important; Old Georgio had carefully explained that when he had read out the newspaper story and several of the younger women of the village had been frightened, and Old Georgio had reassured them that, "It only happens to the very rich, for, after all, who would profit from kidnapping a poor man?" Luca giggled. 'Kidnapping', it had seemed such a funny word at the time, and it still did. Yet people grew wealthy from it. All those days and nights on the hill Luca had pondered it; all the other things in the newspaper story he knew he could do but how, where would he ever come across someone very rich? Luca patted the car, and smiled.

Old Georgio was first into the square that evening. Luca saw him as soon as he breasted the rise and paused for a moment. Old Georgio— and his father! Both sitting there, sipping their wine.

Luca began to run, and as he ran the two sodden bundles he had slung from his waist bumped against his body. He couldn't wait to see Old Georgio's face, but best of all, his father's; no, he wouldn't take him for a fool after this. Not when he found out what Luca had done.

Twenty million lira! It had been easy, much easier than he had imagined. Twenty million lira! He would share it with the whole village of course, he would be looked up to, treated with respect at last.

Twenty million lira. That, Old Georgio had explained, was what the rich people paid when sent their son's ear.

Luca laughed out loud. Twenty million for a single ear! What would the rich people pay for two whole heads!?

TATTOO

FRANK TULLIVER HAD BEEN DRUNK WHEN HE GOT himself tattooed. They had dropped anchor and secured the ship three nights before, it had been a long haul from Valdivia, around the Cape, across to Sierra Leone, and finally through the Straits to Barcelona. Nearly three months at sea with the sickly sweet smells of coffee and bananas and oranges, yes, Frank had been very drunk when he got himself tattooed, and now, as he lay on the beach of Sitges he kept the flat of his hand on his chest and wondered if the tattooist hadn't been drunk too.

Luckily the bar he chose to do his final drinking and fighting in had not been too far from the ship so when the Guardia Civil had been summoned they had found his papers and, perhaps because it was very late and they wanted to quickly go off duty without making out arrest reports, they sent for The Badger. Tom Badgerforth was the grinning and grizzled bosun of the old tub and knew exactly how to deal with young men who had drunk too much Fundador—liberally laced with cheap Spanish Champagne. He didn't take Frank back to the ship, that would have been anti-social since Frank shared quarters with six other men, instead he found him a room with a bed, and a basin conveniently situated nearby, and left him there to sleep it off.

After five or six bouts of terrible retching sickness Frank eventually slept for most of the next day. When he awoke he found himself still dressed except for his shoes and with just a few pesetas in his pocket. He was glad then of the Company rule, they knew all about 'distressed British seamen' and insisted that the men be paid (and after three months at sea, each had a tidy sum) only a comparatively small amount in cash, and the rest deposited with the Spanish branch of a British bank with drawing arrangements made.

Frank's first thought was to strip off his clothes and bathe, but even then it wasn't until he stood trying to coax warm water out of the spasmodic shower at the end of the corridor that he first saw the tattoo. At first he thought it was a bruise from the brawl of the night before, a blueish—greenish mottled mark in the middle of his chest, about the size of the Mercantile badge on Frank's cap, it was sore to touch, and itched like the very devil. But closer inspection revealed the mottling to be a muddled design of some kind, Frank could not really make it out.

Then through the throb of his head he began to remember, vaguely, turning into a narrow street and seeing a lit doorway and then the sign; Frank was furious with himself. Seamen DID get themselves tattooed, yes, it was a tradition, but a fast fading one, even the old salts would look at an 'Elsie' on their arm and think about the 'Beryl' back home! Frank had never yet met a seaman who hadn't been three points to the wind when he got tattooed, and bitterly regretted it afterwards.

He wondered what Suzy would think of it. Suzy was the girl Frank hoped to marry and they had planned that, during his leave, during the long stop-over at Barcelona, she would fly out to join him. He was worried about what Suzy might think. Then he again looked at the tattoo and wondered what on earth it was supposed to be, just a squiggle of lines contained within a circle, and *that* was imperfectly drawn too! Then Frank remembered that he had heard somewhere that tattoos *could* be removed, a painful process, but after all this one wasn't too big; after thinking that Frank felt a whole lot better.

Frank had booked two rooms at the Miramar Hotel in Sitges, he knew that Suzy would agree, would expect to share his bed throughout their stay, but she always insisted on two rooms 'because it looks better'.

The Miramar was at the northern end of the town, about where the town began in fact, and sat in the shadow of the beautiful old church with its tiny belfry and charming custom of, instead of striking the hour at mid-day, piping a recording of classical music; it was an odd and wonderful sensation the first time you heard it, the concealed speakers were pointed out to sea so that the wind caught the beautiful strains of Bach or Beethoven, and brought them back across the beach, ethereal music, seeming to come from nowhere and yet you constantly turned, half expecting to see a philharmonic orchestra floating off shore.

Suzy was due to arrive later in the day and Frank was worried again, not just about what Suzy might say, but also because the tattoo had obviously been executed by a very inferior craftsman indeed. The ink was running, Frank had thought it might be his imagination, but he had measured the damned thing that morning, and again a few hours later, and it was bigger than before so obviously the ink under his skin was running, spreading in some way. Frank thought it might have something to do with the effect of the sun, and now lay on the beach with a scrap of tissue over the tattoo, glued in place with sun-tan lotion. He felt ridiculous.

Suzy could not have done a worse thing; he had met her at the airport and brought her back by cab. On the way, there had not been an opportunity to mention the tattoo, Suzy, who had never been to Sitges before, was excited and enchanted by the winding, hair-pinned road clinging to the cliff face with spectacular views of the Mediterranean far below. About half way there is a regrettable cement works, and from a distance Frank kidded Suzy that it was their hotel looming up. Then they rounded the final bend and Sitges was spread out ahead of them, the Terramar Hotel, with its tiered rooms, looking exactly like a wedding cake. Frank wished they were staying there.

But Suzy loved the Miramar with its tiny walled garden and citrus trees, and he suggested that she have a drink before going to her room. They sat sipping Tequila Sunrises and watching the world go by, and that is when Suzy did it. A powerfully muscled lifeguard, bronzed and wearing just shorts walked by, down his arms and across his chest were several large tattoos. Suzy made a mouth, "What a fool," she said, "How could a man ruin himself like that—permanently too!"

Frank guiltily glanced down the front of his open neck shirt and was shocked to see his tattoo. It couldn't be, it was in such a position that he could only see it in a mirror, or by tucking his chin right in, but he could see it, stretching down almost to his navel now.

It was changing colour too, Frank was glad of the two rooms now because while Suzy was unpacking, he had slipped into his own room and stripped off his shirt. The tattoo was now larger than the span of his hand, and touches of red were beginning to appear in the pattern.

He heard Suzy calling him and quickly put his shirt back on again.

That night they made love in the dark, and the next morning he pretended a bad headache and sat in the shade, his shirt on and buttoned while he watched Suzy swim and play in the surf.

They made love in the dark again that night, and before that, when they were each getting ready for dinner, Suzy had knocked at the door of his room, and been surprised to find it locked and he had made the excuse that the lock was faulty, but clearly it could not go on like this. Already, over dinner, Suzy had studied him and then said, "You've changed, since the last time, or you're worrying about something and haven't told me." Worrying about something? Frank only slept fitfully that night, with Suzy in his arms, and him thinking that he might over sleep and it would be light already, and Suzy would wake up first and sit up in bed and look at him and . . . He was awake at first light, wondering if he had really slept, and then he was up and dressed and forcing a smile for Suzy and persuading her that they shouldn't go to the beach that day, they should take one of the coach trips to the Monastery at Montseraat, The Monastery was inland, high in the mountains, and the air was chill; Frank could wear his shirt, buttoned to the neck.

The day was only a partial success, at the Monastery they made a sweet heady liquor and were liberal with free samples so Frank felt easier after a while, more relaxed. But Suzy kept regarding him curiously and then, on the way back in the coach, she suddenly asked him, if he was "going off her?" Frank protested, that was very far from the truth, and she in turn levelled the accusation that he seemed far away, thinking possibly of someone else. They came perilously close to a row, but that evening, before he put on the soft silk high necked sweater he had rushed into the town and bought specially (Taking great care to buy her something too) he looked at himself in the mirror. The ink did not seem to have spread any further.

Before dinner they ate olives and little rolls of marinated squid in a bodega up near the main road, where crouched old ladies in black brought straw wrapped bottles to be filled from oak casks standing like enormous soldiers in the gloomy recesses at the rear—they took their chilled wine and sat at one of the few tables outside, in a narrow, cobbled, sharply descending street where from time to time large polished bricks rose up from the middle of the thoroughfare to point to a place where mules could be stopped and rested, or prevented from running away pell-mell to the promenade below.

Frank was happy, he had forgotten; until Suzy leaned forward and wondered if the sun hadn't brought up a rash on his neck, "Just there, above your collar, looks red and nasty." Frank pulled the collar higher, and now could not wait for the evening to end, so that he might inspect himself in the privacy of his bathroom.

They did not make love that night, and Frank wondered if it were not too hot for them to share a bed? Suzy looked at him in a funny way, but eventually, just a few pecks and kisses later, she retired to her own room.

The thing had spread frighteningly in every direction, a blush of curls and colour now suffused his whole torso, and tendrils of it had invaded his thighs, and crawled down his arms as far as his elbows; he knew, now that he had to seek expert advice, or the tattooist, or both. It would be difficult, to summon a doctor to the hotel, or slip away and consult one in the village, it would be very difficult to do it without arousing Suzy's suspicions, but he thought of a way and quietly left the hotel room.

It WAS very hot that night and what little sleep he got was lying naked on top of the bed. A pale sun awakened him early and for one shocking moment he thought a snake was lying on his pillow close to his face, then he realised it was his own arm. The pattern had reached the white strip where his wristwatch had shielded him from the sun, but there was a difference this time, where before the pattern had merely ended in a mass of squiggles—the way a child who cannot yet write mimics a signature—this time there was a shape to the termination; five little knobs of colour pointing down, towards his fingers.

The cable arrived while they were at breakfast, a short, terse message summoning him back to his ship, "Probably haven't logged the stores properly," Frank said lightly, quickly folding the cable in his hand before Suzy might spot the office of origin, because Frank had sent the cable to himself the night before, from the desk of a nearby hotel. He assured Suzy that he would be back within twenty-four hours, and then went up to his room to pack the smallest of bags, and to take one last look (he couldn't help himself) at his body in the mirror.

He sat deeply in the corner of the cab, avoiding the eyes of the driver in the rear view mirror, and holding a handkerchief to his mouth as though he had a toothache. It had been his intention on reaching

Barcelona to go straight to a doctor, but now he instead directed the cab to one of the big stores and there, still holding the handkerchief against his face, he bought two large bottles of pancake make-up, several rolls of bandages, a pair of linen gloves and some sunglasses, the biggest he could find. He then checked into a cheap hotel down near the dockside.

The wardrobe mirror was cracked and flyblown, and he had the shutters closed, so a full inspection took some time; the tattoo now covered the whole of his body—save for one tiny patch at his back—and when he removed the linen gloves it was to find that he now wore other gloves beneath; like the finest snakeskin, curls and roundels of pattern extending even under the fingernails, the soles of his feet too had been embraced by it. The face that stared back at him was like the face of a cowboy robber he had seen in films as a child; a kerchief of elaborate design, pulled up to just above the nose. He picked up one of the bottles of make-up and began to shake it.

He did not venture out of the hotel until it was quite dark, and then down the back stairs. He had clumsily bandaged his throat and chin and wore the dark glasses; the caked make-up glowed pinkly on his nose, across his forehead and around his eyes, but even so the pattern of the tattoo still faintly showed through.

He had found the doctor's address, in the phone book and now, seeking the side roads where-ever possible, and the shadows within them, he made his way there. The surgery was shut, but there was an emergency bell, Frank reached up and unscrewed the bulb over the porch before he rang the bell.

The doctor was tetchy and Frank's Spanish poor, keeping well back into the shadows, he managed to explain a "Skin infection"; the doctor grunted, then turned away and Frank followed him down a dim and narrow corridor to a consulting room, here, under a hard white, unshaded light, the doctor turned and looked fully at Frank for the first time, and stared. Then, indicating a linen screen, he asked Frank to strip.

Frank was never to forget that the doctor stood and regarded Frank's naked body in horror, and then crossed himself. And then reached for the hypodermic.

Frank ran. Ran through dark and sometimes cobbled streets, he knew he could not go back to the doctor, nor could he ever go back to Suzy and Sitges, but he was a seaman with a seaman's instincts, he knew he was running towards the dockside and the sea. The bandages had slipped now so that when Frank grabbed a passer-by and asked about the tattooist's the man squealed in fear and then, backing for the first few steps, turned and ran away, Frank tried to retrace the journey of that drunken evening only a few days before, he found a bar that seemed familiar, and then an alleyway, and then the blindman. "A tattooist?" the blind man frowned for a long moment until Frank put a coin into his plate, "Ah, yes, there is . . . or there was a tattooist, just down there, I don't know if he is still there, I haven't seen him in a long while," Frank left the blindman rattling his plate and still laughing at his little joke.

He saw the doorway as soon as he turned the corner, but it was unlit, he hurried closer then stood in despair as he saw the rough wood boards clumsily nailed across the door and window, and just here and there faded lettering telling of "Tattooing." Frank ran his hands over the boards, it couldn't be! The place looked as though it had been empty, shut up for years, and yet that couldn't be!

Then Frank thought he saw a light deep within the interior of the shop, a tiny flicker of flame like a guttering candle, or a match suddenly struck; he pressed his face closer, to peer between the boards and his own eyes glared back at him and—yes—for a moment there seemed to be a flame dancing in them. He remembered then, vaguely, far off, the Spanish of the blindman, and some words he did not fully understand, "Nikki antiquitie," that had been the tattooist's name, Old Nikki, Old Nick.

Frank remembered too why he had run from the doctor's house; the doctor had seen him as a monster, something terrible to be destroyed, crossing himself he had reached for his hypodermic, and Frank's hands, such wonderfully strong hands now, had clamped around the doctor's throat and . . . he felt a tiny twinge of regret as he thought of Sitges and Suzy, and why he could never go back there. She should have knocked, should not have just opened the door and walked in while he was standing there before the mirror. She should not have screamed either, not like that, as though he were not Frank, as though she did not know him.

That was when he had first realised how strong his hands had become. It was a twinge, just a twinge of regret as he thought of Suzy, but he would never think of her again.

The board was smouldering now, glowing red where Frank's breath had been beating upon it. Frank smiled, it would soon be a raging fire, a *beautiful* inferno. There was an impish bounce in his step now, everything was coming out right, everything would be complete, even his body which was covered from head to toe with the tattoo—except for that one tiny patch at his back, a little round circle, no bigger than a fifty peseta coin, but then, as Frank rightly theorised, eventually his tail would cover that.

Continuing Saga

I REMEMBER ONCE FINDING A BEE IN THE BATHROOM but I didn't kill it. Well I hate killing things and especially bees who seem to do nothing but good in this world and whose sonorous buzzing heralds Spring for me as much as does the call of the cuckoo. This bee was trapped against the furthest window, the one that didn't open and was divided into half a dozen panes. Bees are stupid creatures in some respects, or perhaps their field of vision is limited, but anyway once trapped against a window they just keep flying at the light they can see, frequently to end up dead of exhaustion with an open window and freedom just a few inches away. I suppose it took me about ten patient minutes to manoeuvre the bee, with the edge of a magazine, across the several panes of the window. Several times it would evade my touch, fly briefly, and end, up right back where it had started and I would have to begin all over again. Finally however my efforts were rewarded, I gave it a quick flip that took it around the window jamb, and it flew out of the open window. A swallow from the nest overhead swooped down and ate it in mid-flight.

I felt as I did then as I watched the Old Man tear up the lay-out I had sweated and wasted the entire week-end on, "It lacks zing." The Old Man was a 'Sir', wore an Old Harrovian tie and was as British as they come, right down to his Lobb shoes, but he occasionally used the odd American word. Usually ten years after they were no longer popular parlance. Advertising is like that, a very funny business populated with a cross section of very funny people, many of them highly talented, all of them, if they would admit it, extremely guilt ridden. It's the nature of the craft, and yes it is a craft, has to be, because is not the word 'craft' only a 'y' away from 'crafty'? Deep down we know our parasitic role and so we compensate; "Advertising is a phenomena to the social good, it HELPS society," completely ignoring that society got on very well without it thank you very much for only about a couple of million years. "We understand peoples' dreams," well that too, but more important we understand their foibles and weaknesses and are quick to exploit them. Brain washing was not perfected in a KGB cellar but on Madison Avenue.

As the Old Man tossed the remains of my layout into his waste paper basket it seemed a bad time to choose to tell me that a new man was joining my department, nevertheless I don't think it coloured my attitude later on.

I hated him from the moment he arrived. And he hated me. It was a completely irrational hate because he was indeed a very pleasant, handsome young man, and that description would fit me too. Nor was he a threat to seniority, after all he was merely replacing Jock, and we would both be working under the Controller in circumstances of utter equality. Yet we hated each other instantly. His name was Guy Gisbee, and he came from Nottingham. That in itself should have assured a smooth opening gambit because, right up until my grandfather's time, my own family had lived in that area; not in the city, but close to the leafy green of Sherwood. Gisbee confessed that, despite living so near, he had never once ventured into the Forest.

If the Americans did not actually invent advertising they certainly refined it and laid down certain ground rules which many of the big companies still abide by; one is that creative people should not be confined in individual offices, but rather should stimulate and feed off each other in one communal space. At least that's the theory, although what it actually means is just another committee; either the Americans are the most gregarious people on earth or they do just love the committee with its subjugation of radical thought and levelling of everything to the lowest common norm—which might well explain the Ford Edsel, most of their television product and, who knows, the camel?

In practice it means that most of one's better work is done quietly, in the privacy of one's own home, and the rest of the week one's style is cramped by having to work cheek by creative jowl with one's colleagues. Gisbee had the desk next to mine.

Gisbee had been assigned to the 'Image' accounts or, as we term them, the 'Jollies'. These are advertisers who did the hard sell on their products yonks ago, and can now sell just about as much of their stuff as they can manufacture but nevertheless still worry that their profit margin this year might slip below the billion, and therefore want to keep their brand name in the public eye. The result is advertising that doesn't sell anything, just a name, and usually in such a way that it is jokey and jolly, and makes you feel 'real warm and good inside'—a bit like a favourite uncle come to stay. They are great fun to work on because to a certain degree one's imagination is unreigned, certainly without the fetters of laboriously explaining what the product does, and why it should be bought in preference to another product that does exactly the same thing—sometimes better.

I did not resent relinquishing the 'Jollies' to Gisbee, after all I had been on them for more than two years and that is a long time to feel jolly. Not only that, I was on 'Dreams' now. 'Dreams' is when you take something very mundane . . . like a fisherman's boot, and fill it with delicious leg. Well, how would YOU sell a fisherman's boot?! The layout artist of course is often taken along on location when they are shooting the TV commercials and there you have the adman's lore of 'the furthest distance between two points'. In essence this means that if, for instance, your fisherman's boot is made in Grimsby and, one hopes, most of the potential buyers will come from similar seaports, you shoot the commercial if not in Timbuktoo, then certainly Thailand. Filled with that delicious leg. Or legs—you see, not only was I on 'Dreams', but on 'Aperitif Dreams'. I had to almost fight off the other boys with a big stick to get that assignment, but they weren't too upset about it because no-one gets 'Aperitif Dreams' for longer than a year at the most. Any longer than that and blood pressure creeps to danger levels. 'Aperitif Dream' commercials are like those big, big old Hollywood movies. Except that they cost a lot more.

They are ALWAYS set in the most fabulous flesh and sun spots of the world, and no 'Aperitif Dream' worth a sip would have less than about six beautiful girls per commercial. Plus two or three male models with muscular jockstraps, but most of *them* are no threat, so that leaves the crew, and the layout artist. I don't know about blood pressure, but I think a man could go blind.

I consciously resented Gisbee getting 'Aperitif Dreams' some day. For the first week, apart from pointing him to the restaurant and other necessary doors, I said very little to him, but then a new breakfast cereal hit the market and the one we represented panicked. Gisbee and me were seconded to a 'brain-storming' session, the object of which was the counter attack of OUR breakfast cereal, 'Brain storming', like 'person- alised', is an American invention. And about as silly; I mean if a man doesn't know it's HIS shirt and HE'S inside it well what is the world coming to? 'Brain-storming' is an extension of word association; about a dozen selected brains are put into a room, drink is made available (that is the only good part) and the one line problem is put; "How to sell soap" Or cereal in this case. After that you are on your own, you can say just whatever comes into your head. Except expletives, the whole nonsense is tape recorded and what with the Old Man being a Harrovian and all, expletives are strictly taboo. Although they might often make more sense then what does come out; "A ship" someone might say, "A liner" someone else, and then, "Let's fill the Queen Mary with cornflakes!" We get paid for it too.

I don't play. Or at least I cheat, I'm a great tennis fan you see, so I usually think about what ever tournament is going on around the world somewhere, so they are likely to get "Love" or "Forest Hills" or "Umpire" from me, although there was one time I said "Balls," and they stopped the tape and wound it back and gave me some very hard looks.

It was different this time because Gisbee was there. We were seated across from each other and somehow I couldn't think of tennis. The others rambled on about new packaging, new slogans, but Gisbee and I just sat there and glared at each other. Then it was his turn and he said, "Kill." The others took him at his word, did he mean an 'overkill campaign'? Or should they try to kill the image of the rival product? I just sat there and looked at him, and I knew. Then it was my turn, "From way back." I startled myself, that hadn't been in my mind, in fact I had formed something quite different to say, some- thing facetious, but, "From way back"? I didn't know what it meant, neither did Gisbee, yet somehow it meant *something* to both of us. The others seized upon it, "way back"! Yes! The new product was an upstart, whereas OUR cereal had been around since granny was a boy, or something like that.

A campaign that exploited grass roots and years of tradition, and that was to do everything asked of it began right there from a remark I had made but did not understand. It was the first and only time I had known anything positive and resolute come out of a brain storming session.

That evening I invited Gisbee to come for a drink. He accepted, I knew he would because the whole situation was damned ridiculous and we had to bring it out into the open. Not right away though, we sat and drank and spoke of other things and I found out that, like me, he was a tennis fan too; his father was actually a member at Wimbledon and was allocated Centre Court tickets, so not only should I have liked him, but cultivated him! It wasn't to be because after he had finished the drink I had bought him and meticulously bought me one in return, he said, "You hate me," and then added, "And I hate you." Then it was my turn to talk, "Why?" and I really meant it, why?!

Gisbee smiled, and I loathed him even more, "I don't know, chemical reaction do you think?" He went on, expounding various theories, very charming, very pleasant and I could have cheerfully smashed his face in. He grew edgy, his eyes flicking up and down me as he spoke, despising everything he saw. His hands too were nervous, strong hands that kept making fists, we eventually parted, with nothing solved and the way we had started, mortal, malevolent enemies.

There is a certain breakfast food contained in a giant sized packet, and yet when you open it the plastic bag inside, the bag that actually holds the cereal, is much, much smaller. There is no question of short weight the various standards boards would not allow that, and yet there IS a trick involved, a very carefully worked out trick. The outside packet is the key, nicely gauged to a centimetre so that it just WON'T go into the average shopping basket, which means that the housewife who buys it—and there are millions, I promise you—has to balance it on top of her basket or carry it in her hand. So everywhere she walks, which is more than likely to be a lot of other shops, she is advertising the product free! You just can't get away from it. It was the same with Gisbee, it seemed for the next few weeks we kept bumping into each other, not just at work, that was inevitable, but socially, at the same parties, in the same pubs, and once in the same tailors, and twice at the same disco. Fate was working in mysterious ways.

Work was reasonably congenial, by tacit agreement we would say very little to each other while in the office. Sometimes my eyes would crawl from my paper knife to his exposed back, and once I caught him doodling lots of little dead men, all speared with something suspiciously like the leg of the tripod easel that sat between us, but otherwise there was relative calm. The Junior Executive's Men's room was another thing altogether, we frequently found ourselves washing our hands in there just before or after lunch, and alone. Then I would speak to him as I really felt, "You . . . " I would say, but I never completed the dots because no one was ever quite sure just where the jurisdiction of the Old Man's tape recorders ended. Just, "You . . . " but it was enough, Gisbee understood, "One of these days," he would retort, "One of these days I'm going to break your greasy neck!" Gisbee had originally started as a copy-writer, and I suspect an inferior one. Flowery, and inaccurate too, because whatever my neck was, it was NOT greasy. It became a point of honour to top him, "Just breaking YOUR neck would be too good for you," I'd reply. "No, I want to stick something sharp and jagged in your guts and turn it, and watch you squirm." Then we'd both nod, faintly smile, and go back to work.

I didn't really appreciate what it was doing to me. That's possible, in fact the science of advertising is built upon just such a premise; there is a story, possibly apocryphal, about an American Railroad back in the Thirties; apparently it was a terribly ghastly railroad (and perhaps the forerunner of the railway system we have in this country now), it was dirty, never ran on time, the stations were falling down. Disaster, etcetera. Worst of all it was losing money. So the big-wigs of the company scraped together their last few hundred thousand and came to see an Advertising Sage, "Save us," they begged, "Save us from the ungrateful commuters who are turning to their automobiles, and away from our Railroad just because it is terribly ghastly. Give us An Image." The Sage was honest, I'll, say that for him, but he was also devious. He took their money and spent not a cent on newspaper advertising, not a cent on radio jingles urging the lost commuters to come back to their railroad. No, all he did was put up some big posters, only on the stations. "This Railroad," said the posters, "Is the Best in The World." The Finest, The Most Efficient, The Most Punctual, The Cleanest . . . and so on.

The commuters, standing wondering if Tuesday's train would get there by Wednesday, and knowing that when it DID arrive they would sit on spilled horsehair and God's knows what else, and that even then the train might never reach its destination, the commuters laughed. They openly sneered, and some even added remarks of their own to the posters—especially the one that promised, "We Strain For Better Things."

Yet miraculously the Railroad began to improve, become more efficient, cleaner, sharper, as the Sage had known it would. You see *he* had realised that it is not the commuter who sets the standard, but the staff! The posters had never been aimed at, never intended for the commuter, but always for the staff. They, after all, stood under the shadow of those posters all day, they read them, the message sunk into their subconscious and gradually they thought, "By God, someone believes in us!" and then, "If this IS the best railroad in the world I'm working for, then I'd better look like it, *work* like it!" Apocryphal or not it is a good summation of advertising at its best, of the power behind it, and the fact that, resist it, like it or not, we can be directed and motivated by pre-ordained forces.

Mary said that. Well, not quite like that, she's far too direct to monkey about with words. What she did say, in a nutshell, was that it was probably MY fault this thing between me and Gisbee. *I* had got off on the wrong foot, not liking him for whatever deep seated reasons, and that HE in return had become infected by my attitude and was just standing firm, retaliating, as any red blooded man might. I could just about EAT Mary whenever she says 'red blooded man'. The upshot of it was that she insisted on meeting Gisbee.

I hesitated about that, Mary was my domain, or at least she had been until about a year ago when her father had whipped her off to South America to look at Aztec murals. I was never quite sure whether the object of the exercise was to look at murals, or not look at me. Anyway it worked, before then I'd been mucking her about a bit I suppose, living with her on and off, but still sowing oats across most of the Home Counties. While she had been away I had missed her more than I thought possible. And now she was back, and I was quite sure about us. I really didn't care anymore if or when they took me off 'Aperitif Dreams'. Being in love does strange things to a man, it even allows him to introduce the girl he loves to the man he hates.

It was a mistake. Mary had only been back in my life a couple of weeks and SHE was still a bit unsure or, on reflection, might have been teaching me a lesson. At any rate, she took to Gisbee, fawned over him. And he? Well, it was like the reuniting of star crossed lovers as far as he was concerned. I knew he loved her, coveted her, wanted her with the same intensity, the same *passion* that he hated me. Perhaps it was just that as far as Mary was concerned, a woman flattered and responding to a man who quite obviously was totally bowled over by her. What woman could resist an opportunity like that? Mary didn't.

Dinner had been Mary's idea, so I had settled on the Villa de Cesare on the logic that, when I got tired of looking at him I could always look at the river. We had a table on the balcony, with the dance floor below; and that is where I sat most of the evening, on the balcony, gazing down at Mary and Gisbee dancing below. Mary later said (well actually she shouted it), that she was just being polite, dancing more with him than with me, but I didn't like it. They both knew I didn't like it, but they bloody well went on doing it just the same damn them!

There was a moment, a quite incomprehensible moment while I watched them and I looked desperately for a rope, a rope I could grab, swing down on, and snatch Mary from his arms and carry her away across the draw-bridge. Yes, draw-bridge, I actually thought that. Mind you, The Villa de Cesare is a film director's cross of Ancient Rome and Ye Olde Merrie England.

As they came back to the table together I wished I'd ordered steak; they give you those sharp little serrated knives when you order steak. If I had been the wallpaper I'd have got more attention, someone sooner or later comments on the wallpaper, don't they? They sat and talked and looked at each other and Mary laughed a lot, and now I noticed in him something I had not seen before, a superciliousness, a charm spread too thick, a self congratulatory triumph. The man was positively oily, and had the nerve to refer to my neck as 'greasy'.

Happily though it degenerated into a very unhappy evening; the barbs were out and Mary was in the middle, she wouldn't be suggesting any more dinners with Gisbee along. That was the second mistake of the day. I had never bothered to find out exactly where Gisbee lived, probably for fear that I would be impelled to slip round there one night and choke the life out of him! It turned out that he lived just around the corner from Mary and, I'll never know quite how it happened, I found myself standing like a lonely lemon on the Chelsea Embankment watching Mary drive away with Gisbee. He hadn't even offered to split the bill! I knew then not that I could kill him, but that I was going to. That was the only thing that kept me sane as I drove home alone, thinking of various painful ways of disposing of Gisbee.

I am not one of those men who lets a woman dominate, no, I'm one of the old school of 'treat 'em rough—love 'em and leave 'em'. I called Mary the next morning as soon as decently possible at 6.30. She was sleepy of course and for a moment her voice formed a "Guy," or the beginning of it; I kept very calm and asked her out that evening. She told me she was busy. Then I didn't keep calm, I began to bluster I suppose, and she hung up on me, and then didn't even bother to answer when I rang back immediately.

Gisbee whistled a lot in the office that day and sometimes when he caught me looking at him, his eyes would smile. Just his eyes. I doodled a lot of little dead men that day.

Of course I followed them. From Mary's place to a pub, then a chic little restaurant, then back to Mary's place again. I was going to kill him there and then, only one thing prevented me, I had a very special demise in mind for Mr. Gisbee and, although these days you can get most things in the King's Road there are still a few you can't get. One of them is boiling oil in large quantities.

The next day I didn't go into the office, I had to go to a photographer's studio in Fulham to O.K. some models. I had cabbed there and later, the tallest and most beautiful of the girls and one of those I had agreed we should use, looked at me with a glint of gratitude and offered me a lift. I turned her down, so you can see what a bad way I was in.

I decided to walk back across Hyde Park and then, about halfway I suppose, I must have got the blackout. Certainly I have no recollection of climbing the tree, but that is where I found myself, crouched about mid-way amongst the leafy branches of a tall tree. Then some kids spotted me and began to shout up at me, and I saw a blue uniform strolling closer and I scrambled down the tree and hurried home.

I did not try to call Mary that night, and although MY phone rang several times I did not answer it. I lay huddled on my bed and thought; Gisbee had done me a favour, he had taken my unfounded instinctive hate for him and crystalised it, given it reason, given it purpose. I wished I was back in that tree again, trees are good places to hide, and to plan.

The next day was Saturday and indeed, if some of the other boys from the office hadn't come to collect me I would have forgotten about it altogether. As it was they had to hang around grumbling while I got shaved and ready, and we were late. The thing had started when we arrived.

Public Relations, or 'PR' is a natural advertising off-shoot and squarely based on the precept that, 'if you say something often enough *somebody* is going to believe it'. It began as news bending, "Play up the fact that the factory is going to bring more *jobs* to the area" and play down the angle that the toxic fumes will probably kill them all!" But it has moved on since then, become big business, so that now anyone who is anyone has his or her own PR man, much as they used to have analysts. It can be delicate work, and hazardous; a PR man usually drinks too much or not at all, mainly because a great deal of his job is dropping antidote (being the opposite of poison) into journalistic ears, and journalistic ears are notoriously widened when in the presence of superb food, beautiful women and, most important of all, a good bottle of Beaune, preferably '65, preferably TWO bottles. The success of a PR man is not always predictable, he may spend all afternoon at lunch, and most of the evening in a club persuading a journalist that to mention that the pimply daughter of some asset stripping millionaire "likes horses and children and wants to spend her whole life looking after them" would make for fascinating news ... apart from which it might help to counteract that nasty story last week, where she was found naked with a negro, a Guardsman and an under gardener, doped up to her armpits and wearing a Mars bar in a most avant garde location! The PR man convinces the journalist, perhaps favours are exchanged, and next day there isn't a whisper in the paper because it ran out of space, because, as the PR man puts it, "That Son of a B of a President just HAD to go and get assassinated on a MONDAY, didn't he?"

There are other pitfalls; like the PR man who was assigned to a famous personality about whom there were rumours—all of them true— that he was a homosexual, and the PR man's task was to make sure that there were never, NEVER any photographs allowed depicting the personality in juxtaposition with other members (if you will forgive the phrase) of the male sex. He did pretty well too, then let slip a photo which showed the personality standing beaming, and behind him someone had raised a banner saying, "The man who's always right behind us."

Our company indulges in a little PR too, gentle stuff on our own behalf. Once a year we have a Sports Day, it is not just potato races and Donkey Derbys, although there are a few of those too, but it is more of a Fete; there are stalls and sideshows and marquees, and a few famous people generously donate (for a handsome fee) their presence to the proceedings, and at the end of the day a fat cheque is presented to a worthwhile cause. OUR PR man sees to it that the name of our company is printed much larger on the cheque than the name of the cause.

It does us some good I suppose, and it certainly does not do the cause any harm. Junior Executives such as me are expected to turn out and wander around with fixed grins and grab anyone who looks miserable and persuade them that they ARE having a good time really!

I usually like the occasion because the Variety Club always sends along two dozen specially selected chorus girls—specially selected I always think because they never QUITE fit the abbreviated costumes they wear and circulate in, acting as kind of cheer leaders for the event. In the past I have always narrowed the Variety Club's short list of twenty four down to one, and taken her home. This time I could only think of Mary. And the dreadful Gisbee. The Fete, which this year was being held in the grounds of a grand old stately home, was spread out over several acres and there were a lot of people. Even if Gisbee were here (and I wasn't sure that he even knew about the event) I might not bump into him, but just thinking about him made me catch my breath and my face grow hot.

I needed a drink, but so it would seem, did half a hundred others; I stood in the hot, airless tent waiting for a space to appear at the over crowded bar. I didn't get my drink, because at that moment the Old Boy put his head into the tent and looked around for the nearest Junior Executive, "Lockley," he called. I was the nearest. I moved over to him and his voice softened, became wheedling, "Do me a favour, Robin old chap, help Masters out." Masters? I'd never heard of him. "Well actually he's my gardener, came along to help out, gone to a lot of trouble and hardly anyone's gone near his stall," he was steering me now, out of the tent and around the back of it, "Just over there, help him out, drum up some trade. After all that's what our business is all about, isn't it?," he laughed and gave me a little shove in the right direction.

There were two kids, a canoodling couple and a very austere lady sampling the side show, and Masters himself, a thin, perpetually sad man who looked ridiculous, and what was worse KNEW he looked ridiculous. It probably seemed a good idea at the time, to dress up in the long peaked hat the doublet and hose and the coat of Lincoln green, because Masters was running an archery range. About 40 yards away, with straw bales buttressed up behind them, were three archery targets, and Masters stood behind a sagging rope holding a bow and a bunch of arrows. I glanced around, situated as it was behind the tent, and tucked away at that, there didn't seem much chance of drumming up further trade, so I thought I would show willing and have a go myself. Masters didn't know I was an 'inside man', his interest quickened as he took my money and handed me the bow, "Done it before, sir?" No, I hadn't. "Well, sir, it looks easy, but it isn't, you put the arrow to the bow like so . . ." He quickly adjusted my inexperienced hands around the bow and arrow, "Just have a few pulls first, sir, get the feel of it." I did. "Well, that's very good, sir, very good, you're a natural, sir." Ordinarily I would have taken a remark like that as salesman's flattery, but strangely enough the bow DID feel easy in my hands. Familiar.

I grinned, "Well, my name IS Robin," and I drew the bow taut and started to aim at the gold of the target. That's when I heard Mary laugh.

Still holding the bow taut, I turned just a fraction and saw them. Mary and Gisbee, they were some way away, behind and to the left of the straw bales. They were walking but even as I saw them, they stopped and he leaned against a tree, and arched his body out, and pulled Mary towards him.

I stared at Gisbee through the string of the bow, across the tip of the arrow. Later I said it was an accident and Masters supported me, sheer fluke, he would say, that an arrow should carry so far, and so straight. Oh, yes, I was deadly accurate. The arrow flew from my bow and while the 'twang' of its releasing still hung on the air the arrow struck Gisbee and then imbedded itself into the tree behind him. Deeply.

He turned in shock, then gripped the cheek I had scratched but might so easily have laid open, then his eyes lifted across that space and found me. He knew now, as I had known at the moment I had released the arrow, like deja vu suddenly spanning across the centuries. All was clear now, my hate, his hate, and Mary; I knew now that Mary was mine, would always be mine, and no one, least of all Gisbee could ever take her from me.

I took another arrow and fluidly now, to the manner born, I fitted it to the bow, bent and stressed it, and as I came up to the aim he knew that yet again, I had defeated him. He pushed away from the tree, and without a glance at Mary began to walk away very quickly. He didn't look back.

I tossed the bow back to Masters and began to swagger across the grass towards the shocked and bewildered Mary. She would never believe it, so I would never tell her, but HE knew and that was enough.

It had always been there to fathom. Robin Lockley? My grand father had told me many times of how the old gravestones traced back to the time we were once "Loxley and direct descendants of Robin of Loxley— Robin Hood. Guy Gisbee? Those Anglo—Saxons would have corrupted a name like Gisborne to brief Gisbee, wouldn't they? Guy de Gisborne, the scourge of Sherwood, and High Sherrif of Nottingham. No wonder we hated each other, we'd been bred to, it was in our genes.

And Mary? Well 'Mary' isn't a million miles away from 'Marion'. Is it?

WHEN THE TIME COMES

THE BIG BIRD SWOOPED LOW OUT OF THE EAST, out of the rising sun that dappled it pink and orange; for a moment its approach was silent, ethereal, but then the sound of the jet motor caught up with it, preceded it, and then the tyres bit tarmac with a little screech and the bird became an elephant again, a jumbo of the Japanese Airlines.

Not so very far away a small, slit eyed man waited beside a Rolls-Royce that was as white as the suit he wore, as white as the peaked cap he carried under his arm. Long ago his face had crinkled into a permanent grin which, because it WAS permanent, and because it never changed whatever the situation, had become as inscrutable as, utter blankness. Semoi was waiting for Mr. Gregory.

Greg Denver was the last of the passengers to leave the first class section and now he stood for a moment and looked out across London Airport; he was tall and rangy and tanned, and during the long flight there had not been a man or a woman who had not noticed and commented on him; the women with a kind of awed longing, the men to grudgingly agree that, yes, he WAS ruggedly handsome, and yes again, the tiny fleck of grey at his temples DID compliment those beautifully clear blue eyes. The fact that he was an American got some of them wondering that he might be a film star, but that had never been established because throughout the trip he had barely spoken to anyone save for the stewardesses and then perfectly in their own language.

He now spoke again in Japanese as the prettiest of the stewardesses wished that he would have a good time in London. If her eyes held an invitation then Greg did not notice as he thanked her and made his way into the Terminal.

Paradoxically Semoi addressed him in English as he took and loaded his luggage into the Rolls, but Greg knew that Semoi was merely anxious to practice the language.

During the first hour of the drive they spoke very little, except when Greg asked, "Do you think you're going to like it here, Semoi?" And Semoi replied, "My place is with you, Mr. Gregory." "And what about Yasuko?" "Her place is with me." Then later, when the sprawl of city was far behind them and they were travelling through quiet and leafy country roads, Greg started to sit up and take notice, and ask the occasional question; the area was quite new to him, and yet he planned to spend the rest of his life here.

Semoi came to the top of a hill, brought the Rolls to a whispering stop, pointed down and said, "There it is, Mr. Gregory," Greg looked out across green and rolling countryside to where, far in the valley below a large white house stood flanked by forest and trees in its own vast grounds.

It was long and low, a ranch-style one storey affair and the sun winked and flared off big picture windows. Greg looked at it, then nodded, and Semoi drove on, starting to descend the long, winding road to the valley below.

On the way Greg saw a girl riding a horse across a field, she was bare-headed and her long mane of hair flowing out behind her, almost exactly matched the fine chestnut she rode. She reminded Greg of the girls who would come out to ride at his father's ranch and sometimes, because the ranch was very close to the Mexican border, they would run a bull calf or a spirited cow, and Greg would play matador, using his slicker as a cape, often ending up ignominiously in the good, rich earth.

The girl had turned the horse now; and was setting it at a high gate between the hedges, Greg knew it would be a hard and difficult jump, but then trees screened her from sight, and he sat back, wondering if she had made it successfully or not.

Yasuko was waiting by the door of the house to welcome Mr. Gregory, small and smiling and offering him a traditional greeting in Japanese.

The exterior of the house was modern but not alien to a European eye; once inside the vestibule however, Greg slipped off his shoes, slid aside a rice—papered screen and entered Old Japan. Planked wood floors were scattered with rush mats, cushions surrounded a low, oriental table delicately carved from rosewoods; trees in miniature curved exquisitely with pale pastel screens as background, and more sliding doors opened onto other areas of the house. Musk oil (Yasuko knew it to be Mr. Gregory's favourite) hung thinly on the air.

Standing inside the room which was to be Greg's study was Roberts; a gingery, freckled young man wearing a dark suit and looking—and feeling—faintly ridiculous in his bare feet. Yasuko had prepared rose scented saki but Roberts declined it in favour of whisky, then laughed out loud when he found that that too was Japanese! Greg liked Roberts immediately, he was open and eager, out-spokenly honest about the assignment Greg had given him, "I've been an architect for ten years now, and never anything like this." He confessed to spending the first two months just reading about Japanese decor and then—and Greg especially liked him for this—confessed that he might never have got it right if Semoi and Yasuko had not been around to guide and advise him. He was polite too, he respected Greg's privacy; Greg knew he would have dearly liked to ask WHY an American chose to settle in England in a Japanese house. But he didn't.

They sat and chatted for nearly an hour, and then Greg yawned and Roberts remembered the jet lag he must be suffering, and got up to go. Roberts hesitated then, and said, "Look, I don't know how social you intend to be, but I don't live a million miles away, and there is a very good country club nearby, and I'd be delighted to take you along some time, propose you for membership." Greg thanked him ambiguously, and Roberts left.

For the next two weeks Greg stayed in and around the house and grounds; he had found a spot near the road that badly needed clearing, thick shrubs and small elderberry trees had gained a few years of rock-hold, and Greg spent much of the time tearing the shrubs up out of the ground with his bare hands. Yoshi would be arriving soon, and it was good training.

Once, while he was doing this, stripped down to just his Sumo loin-cloth, a sports car drew up on the other side of the hedge, a woman stood up in the car, he glimpsed blonde hair, and heard the woman laugh, and then the car drove on again.

Once too he had seen the girl again, the rider with the long russet hair; he had been high on the hill behind the house and seen her cantering across a field below. He had stood up to see her better, and at that moment she must have become aware of him because she suddenly reined in and turned her face towards his. She had been too far away to be anything but a blur, and later he wondered what she must have made of HIM, because he was wearing the purple kimono Old Nagaski had given him, and it had billowed and eddied in the wind. A vampire? Or a warlock?! Greg had smiled to himself.

At the end of the second week Yoshi arrived; the arena was prepared of course, in fact Greg had had the whole house planned around it, around a square set aside for combat.

Greg never found out what Yoshi REALLY thought of the arrange-ment, in fact it would have been a lapse of honour to even ask—suffice that Yoshi, who was certainly one the three greatest masters of Kendoo in the world (some said the greatest), had agreed to come and live in England and train, and fight against Greg. In return he had accepted one million dollars endowment to his school just outside Hakodadi, and a half a million dollars (in Swiss francs) for himself. Greg knew it was cheap at the price.

He studied Yoshi now as Semoi helped him to buckle on the heavy, pleated breast-plate. A darkly handsome, wonderfully muscled man of about thirty five, about Greg's age. They had been friends for a long time, and yet Friends Eastern-style, Japanese-style, without the shared, man to man intimacies that Greg had had, say, with Bart, his father's foreman, and someone he had been through brawls, booze and brothels with in his time. No, with Yoshi it was the friendship one might have had with a fellow officer on the field of battle, deep, self sacrificing, and yet always with a set of rules, with lines never to be crossed.

Yoshi pulled on the barred mask that so shaded and concealed his face that only the bright white grin of his teeth could be seen; he picked up the hilted wooden sword and moved catlike towards a corner of the arena. Greg hefted his sword through the air a couple of times, moving it very fast so that it sang against the air and he knew, drew Yoshi's unspoken disapproval because he thought such cheap tricks were for tourists and bad movies. Then Greg crouched and splayed his legs, letting the toes of his bare feet seek and consolidate grip on the plain wooden floor. He was ready. They both were ready.

They each took up their terrain, terrain to be defended to the very death, and they faced each other and bowed. Greg had once thought he was a rock, but it was Yoshi who had pointed out that, no, he was a tree, a supple tree, or better still, a blade of grass (for what bends to the wind of attack better than a blade of grass?), immovable because it is rooted to the soil, upright when it chooses to be, yet able to shuck off and ride the strongest storm. Yoshi attacked first, it was his way. And Greg moved into the attack, that was HIS way and, Yoshi had said so many times, that that single action, that *courage*, set him apart from all other Easterners and made him, 'almost Samurai'. The clash of wooden sword upon wooden sword was deafening, it would ring in their ears, that first clash, until the bout was over.

Semoi sat in the vantage of the small gallery and watched as his Mr. Gregory took the great Yoshi back, back to the very edge of his terrain, watched too the feint and blur of stick upon stick, so fast that no human eye could follow it—could they be human who wielded the sticks!? The fight would be long—because only during the fight could Yoshi teach his talented pupil—his normally deep voice becoming strident under stress as he told Mr. Gregory to 'do this' and 'do that'. It sometimes reminded Semoi of the spider and the fly—except that, every time, the fly improved a great deal.

Almost always it would end the same way, the flurry of swords, and then, profoundly, Yoshi's sword would come slashing through Mr. Gregory's expert guard, sometimes a stroke at the side, to remove the heart, still living from the body, sometimes a vicious, upward movement, disembowelling, and *this* time a firm over the shoulder stroke, with all the power that the rooted feet, that the entire body, could command—striking Mr. Gregory across the top of his helmet and, if the helmet were not there, and the wooden swords were steel, surely slicing him into two.

Later Greg and Yoshi sat in the Jakuzi while Yasuko poured the occasional bucket of scented water over their backs, sometimes warm, sometimes piping hot, sometimes icy cold. "This country suits you," said

Yoshi, "You are getting better," and then he grinned a rare grin and, "Or perhaps it does not suit me, and I am getting worse!"

Greg would like to have spoken of the arrangement then, but did not, and when they sat squatted, dry and wrapped in the heavy wool kimonos, drinking saki and dipping tempura into the sizzling pot Yasuko had provided, he again did not mention it.

Greg's karate master was another thing entirely; Japanese yes, and the very best that Britain could provide, but not good enough for Greg, who threw and defeated him half a dozen times, and then philosophically came to think that he must regard *these* sessions as just a work out, an aid to physical fitness. The other things, the spiritual meditation, the 'one-ness', Greg had to find for himself.

It was soon after Yoshi's third visit, when his body felt tight with exertion and every nerve seemed to have crawled nearer the surface, that Greg took the car into town for the first time. He made no exact excuses to himself, he just needed to be away from the house and 'near people' for a little while. The town was not large, and Greg knew that its economy had always depended largely upon farming; once a month cattle were bought and sold there and metal pens were permanently kept in the market square for that purpose. It was an old town with tradition and many of the buildings were two or three hundred years old. Greg liked that, he found a coffee bar where he could sit and look out across the square. He did not seem to be aware of some of the other people in the coffee bar subtly pointing at him and whispering amongst themselves.

It was while he was seated here that he saw her again, for the third time; her long mane of hair was tucked up under a woollen cap but he knew instantly that it was her. She was wearing casual jeans and her legs were almost disproportionately long, and very separate so that they seemed to be socketed in to the corners of her small and trim bottom. Greg only got the merest glimpse of her face, and it was small, pugnacious almost, the nose too tiny, the cheeks too round, not a pretty face, but a very attractive one. Greg watched her as she disappeared into a hairdressers across the square.

He drove home and sat in the Jakuzi, turning the temperature control very briefly to the very hottest and then, for much longer, bringing the stinging underwater jets down to icy coolness. Later, he phoned Roberts.

Roberts was delighted and apologetic in equal proportions, of course he would love Greg to be his guest at the country club, but he had this client to see later on and . . . would Greg mind if he took him there, signed him in? Then came back to collect him later?

The club was much as Greg had imagined it might be, an old building, genuinely old, and now converted so that there were various rooms for billiards, bridge, etcetera, and a softly lit oak beamed bar, with a pleasant restaurant and dance floor adjacent. Roberts added embarrassment to the delight and apologies when they got there, because it WAS early, and only the bar staff were there, and he would have to delay introductions to other members until after he came back. Greg assured him that he could think of nothing nicer than nursing a Scotch at the quiet bar and watching the world go by, and Roberts, leaving explicit instructions that, "Mr. Gregory is MY guest, he must not pay for anything," left him there alone.

Within half an hour the place had filled up considerably and this time Greg WAS aware that he was the subject of many discussions around the club, but particularly amongst a group of young men who had arrived noisily and who had obviously already been to a couple of pubs en route. There was a young woman with them, blonde and with a musical laugh that Greg had heard before. He sat quietly and nursed his second Scotch, and while he nursed it he often caught the young woman's eye (or she his, he was never quite sure), and then those of the young men who seemed to be vying for her attention. He finished his drink and was just debating whether he might have another or slip away leaving a message for Roberts, when the young men approached him and Greg saw now that there were five of them. They were smiling, they seemed friendly, but drink had given an edge to their voices; it began politely enough with introductions being offered, "You're the chap with the new house in the valley, aren't you?" but throughout, the blonde young woman stood in the background her eyes glowing with amusement, "We play rugger." Greg looked at the young man blankly, so then, "Rugger—RUGBY—it's a bit like your American football I suppose, except that WE don't have to cissy ourselves up with all sorts of pads and protectors." Greg smiled and tried to explain that, yes, he had seen both games and that the nature of the American game, with collisions the equal of being hit by a truck or a charging bull, necessitated protective clothing. It was the 'charging bull' that made the young man significantly change his attitude, although it was the 'protective clothing' that he seized upon, "Yes, from what Moira here tells us, YOU could do with some protective clothing, running around the garden in a loincloth." "Like some bloody wog," added another young man, who was thick and squat and powerfully built. They embroidered the accusation now, each of the young men adding to the statement, and each leaning in around Greg until they surrounded him; and still the blonde girl stood in the background, watching. Waiting.

Greg was very quiet now, very still and perhaps that emboldened them; "This is a respectable club, you know." "Don't want your type in here" "Get rid of him, do you think?" At this point the head barman leaned forward, gripped the young man's arm, and uttered a warning. The young man thrust him away, so violently that he hit the rack of glasses behind him and sent one tumbling down.

"Don't do that," Greg's voice was very, very soft, "He's an old man," and he pushed himself up off the bar and looked at them. For the first time, perhaps some self preservation instinct triggered, and the drunken lustre in the young man's eyes cleared. It might have stopped there because already Greg was easing himself away from the bar, but then the blonde laughed, a soft laugh, full of mockery, and the young man grabbed Greg's wrist, "You," he said, "You are just about the right age." Greg looked at the five young men, just five, not so very many, and then, "I'm leaving now." "The Hell you are!" said the young man, and suddenly pushed Greg away into the waiting arms of his friends.

Later on the few other club members who saw the incident would argue about it for hours; some said that only one blow was struck, there could not have been time for more. Others that it had been too quick, the American's hand had moved too quickly to even see the blows, let alone count them. Actually Greg struck four times with the edge of his hand, and once with his elbow. They were economic carefully delivered blows because he had to be quite sure he didn't kill any of the young men. He just taught them better manners, and left them sprawled below the bar, only one of them still conscious. He strolled away then, with the blonde staring after him.

Semoi and Yasuko knew that something must have happened at the club, their Mr. Gregory was in such a strange mood, but they made no comment, nor asked any questions, especially when Mr. Gregory told them to go to bed, but to leave the front door ajar.

Greg had bathed and was just shrugging on the black kimono when he heard the small roar of the sports car. She did not ring the bell but, finding the door open, came straight in. They said very little before, but afterwards, as they lay sprawled across the cushions, she asked him many questions. Greg answered none of them but instead asked her a question, what did she most want at this moment? She laughed and said she had just had everything she needed, but when he persisted she told him that what she most wanted was a new sports car, and she named an exotic name. "You've got it," said Greg, and then got up and left her sitting there, naked and confused.

Greg went to the club again after that (Roberts had made him a member), but not often, just from time to time, and usually in the wake of those days when he an Yoshi met and fought. He never saw the young men again, and only rarely the blonde girl because, although she still followed him with hopeful eyes, there were other girls, many other girls, and his front door was often left ajar. They too asked him many questions but, like the blonde girl before, received expensive gifts, and no answers.

His life at the house was now assuming a tranquil pattern; at first there had been calls and cables and the odd, visit but, at last his colleagues had realised that he had meant it, that he was never again to helm the company that bore his name, and they left him alone.

He had laid out one section of the grounds as a landing field, and he now brought in the tiny Piper, it might just as easily have been the twin-jet Lear, but he wanted a plane only for his own private amusement, and the Piper with its manoeuvreability and low flying speed was perfect for that. The next time he saw the girl with the russet hair it was from the air; it was as he flew low over a copse of trees and came upon the field beyond. He caught the merest glimpse of her and then he pulled the plane round into a tight turn and saw her more clearly; he should have known better, he who had spent all his childhood amongst horses, it reared and became scared and skittish, but she controlled it, and the last he saw of her was her clenched fist raised against him. He climbed away steeply and it was back of his mind that he might, from a reasonable height, follow the girl back to where-ever her house or stables might be, but when he turned and flew back over the area again she was gone.

The next day he drove into town and again sat in the coffee bar; it was a forlorn hope because who could tell how regularly a woman might have her hair done? Or even that she might always choose the same hairdressers? It was a Wednesday, the day before market day and most of the shops closed early at around midday. Greg watched as the hairdressers disgorged the last few of its customers and he got up to leave, and then he saw her. She firmly closed the door of the shop behind her and then carefully locked it, Greg looked again at the sign over the shop, "Diana's." He grinned then as he saw her walk to a battered, shabby Mini, tear the parking ticket from the windscreen and crumple it in her hand. He watched her as she drove away.

Yoshi came that day and they fought. Japanese is a language that has no oathes, no swear words and 'I sincerely hope that you have a very miserable day' is very strong stuff indeed. Yoshi hoped that Greg would have a whole year of miserable days, because he was out of tune, sloppy in his approach, lacking attack and, in a Samurai war would have been dead within the first few seconds.

Greg apologised, clapped his hands for warm saki and they sat and spoke of the old days, not just the old days they had shared together in Tokyo and Hakodadi and Rioto, but the really old days of Ancient Japan, the days that had formed the traditions and protocol that still, despite the industrial and electronic explosion, touched and sometimes governed the lives of many Japanese. Yoshi retold legends that Greg knew but had almost forgotten, he spoke of courtship and betrothal, and finally of the Geisha. Afterwards, when Yoshi had driven away, Greg called Semoi to him and they closed the door on Yasuko, and Semoi too drank saki, and they talked.

Semoi did not find the situation strange, he had acted as intermediary for both his sisters and one brother, no, he did not find it strange, only that this time it involved a European woman. He was, as you would expect him to be, very thorough; the first priority was to confirm the woman's name, and yes, it was Diana, Diana Calvin; the second was find out if she were married or promised—Greg waited tensely for the answers to those questions, but Semoi eventually reported that she had never married and, although she had several boy friends, she was not committed to any. That she was at all musical he was unable to find out, but she DID cook for herself and lived in a small, converted barn about six miles away. Greg and Semoi agreed that it should be there that the initial approach be made. Greg knew that a withdrawal of such a sum from the local bank would not be wise, so instead Semoi drove to

London and brought the money back in a brief case; one hundred thousand pounds in brand new notes.

They chose a Sunday and Semoi took the Rolls to drive those six miles. Greg, guessing that it might be an hour or even two before Semoi returned, stretched naked on the sauna slab while Yasuko walked across his broad back, easing the knots and tensions the day was bringing.

Semoi was back within the hour, his face still blushy red from the slap she had given him and then, before Greg could really question him, the phone rang and he found himself talking to Diana Calvin for the first time. Or, in the main, listening;

"Do you think I'm a whore, is that what you think?"

"Miss Calvin . . . "

"You do think I'm a whore. You're disgusting, disgusting!"

"Miss Calvin, I think you may have misunderstood . . . "

"Your man just came here and offered me a fortune to go to bed with you, what is there to misunderstand about that?"

"Not to go to bed with me," Greg protested, "To *live* with me . . . " but he found himself holding a dead phone.

Semoi tried to soften the blow, the house had been a shambles, her organisation . . . her administration . . . her housekeeping . . . Mr. Gregory was better off without her. But Mr. Gregory wasn't listening, he ran to the plane, fired the engine and took off. For the next two hours he banked and wheeled and dived and did everything save tear the wings off. Then, as the fuel gauge began to flicker, he landed, entered the house and went to sleep, He slept almost through to the next afternoon and Yasuko wanted to awaken him, but Semoi prevented her. Their Mr. Gregory went to the country club that night, but was home earlier than usual and packed them off to bed and left the door ajar.

Yoshi did not wish him any miserable days the next time they fought; on the contrary Yoshi praised him highly for attack, then subtly warned him about emotion, even producing a parable about 'the man who sees not the man he fights, but he whom he *wishes* he could fight, and wins only a surrogate victory, and that is worse than no victory at all'.

Ten days after Semoi got his face slapped he ran urgently to find Greg and tell him that "She is here." She? The Calvin woman!

She was standing looking at the Asangi when Greg entered; he had a momentary feeling of regret that he had chosen to hang the Asangi there because, although the figures were beautifully, exquisitely drawn many Europeans thought the picture pornographic, many Europeans laughed with embarrassment. She neither laughed or smiled, but merely looked at him. Then a smile touched her mouth, a bitter sweet smile as she said, "I just wanted to see for myself," he stared at her, she was wearing the simplest of print dresses that made her seem incredibly innocent and child-like. "To see," she continued," "Just what kind of man would be willing to pay one hundred thousand pounds for this," she made no gesture, just the subtlest movement, the subtlest thrusting forward of her hips. The smile left her now, as she looked into his blue eyes, "I've never been valued so highly," and she turned towards the door.

"No wait!" She paused, and her face was puzzled now. Greg clapped his hands and continued quickly, "It IS a misunderstanding, won't you stay and take saki with me, and at least let me try to explain?"

Yasuko appeared at the door and he ordered saki, and the girl did not move so extending his hand, but not daring to touch her, he lead her deeper into the room to where the cushions were scattered.

He did not wait for her to be seated first but, as any Japanese male would, he plumped himself down and then looked at her. She slowly squatted down on the cushions the other side of the low table. Greg smiled, "It's good for the posture." He waited until Yasuko had poured the saki, placed little porcelain cups before them, and withdrawn, "You are very good to look at. A kimono would suit you," he said. "I am NOT Japanese," she said firmly. "No, if you were you would have understood immediately," he drained his saki cup and as he poured another, "To live with me, be with me, under this same roof, that is all I wanted." "Like a whore!" she snapped. "Like a Geisha!" "A Geisha? That's just another name for a . . ." "No," he interjected, "Perhaps now, perhaps on the Ginza, perhaps since we . . . since the Americans brought their own special culture . . . Yes, there are Geishas who are whores . . . *or whores who say they are Geishas*. . . but the true Geisha, the real Geisha, she is a charming companion, light during a dark day, someone, something, to be looked at and admired, to ease the eyes, to bring perfection, to soothe and delight the senses." She looked at him suspiciously, "The senses? ALL the senses?" Greg shook his head, "No. In the old days, the old way, a man might go elsewhere for that."

She considered for a moment, then leaned forward to recharge her cup, "One hundred thousand, just to be looked at!" "In essence, yes. I would like you to wear the kimono and perhaps do your hair differently, and sometimes cook and serve delicacies, and serve tea traditionally, if you play an instrument that would be nice, if not, then perhaps you might learn . . . and we would talk." She stared at him, "Talk?" He nodded. "Just talk?" she persisted, he nodded again. "And what about . . . well . . . bed?" Greg stood up now, easily, without using his hands, he pushed up and stood tall above her, "I would not touch you, or expect to touch you, that would be part of the bargain." Then he added, "The suite at the back of the house would be yours."

"It's crazy," Greg smiled, "It's unfamiliar. In Japan it would not be at all crazy." She stood up now, "A bargain? What kind of a bargain?" Greg did not understand. "I mean how long does this go on for?"

"I've thought of that" Greg replied, "Normally you would be able to buy yourself out, but that would hardly apply here. I would expect three months notice of your intention to leave, or of course, traditionally, if you were to marry . . ." She laughed then, and Greg liked her laughter although he was bemused by it. "Marry" she said, "Who would I meet to marry, locked up as a prisoner here?"

"You won't be a prisoner," said Greg. "The whole house and grounds." "But" she said, "I wouldn't be allowed out of the grounds?" "I could not stop you, but I wouldn't approve of it. But you may of course have friends over to visit. Female friends."

She paced away and looked at the Asangi again, "Three months" she mused, "One hundred thousand for three months." "I would hope it might be longer, but I would stick by the bargain."

She turned to face him, "Why?" she moved closer to him, "You must at least tell me why?"

"Because," Greg replied, "Japan is a long way away."

The papers were drawn up, first in Japanese by Semoi, and then through an attorney Greg knew. The first document was specific, but the second, at the girl's insistence was ambiguous and appeared to be only a contract of employment. She told the staff of her small shop that she was going away, and left the most senior of them in charge. One week after her first meeting with Greg she moved into his house.

Greg hardly saw her for the first few days, she and Yasuko were far too busy sewing and altering the clothes Greg had had flown over specially, and anyway, just knowing that she was there under his roof made him feel good.

It transpired that she did have a small talent for the piano, but Greg, not wishing so extrovertly European an instrument in the house had bought a tiny harpsichord and had the legs removed so that it now sat on the floor before the cushions. She did not play it the first night they had supper together. There had been something of an entrance when Yasuko shyly ushered her into the room. Greg had approved instantly of the deep green and gold kimono which so perfectly complimented her hair. She had flatly refused the white and pink make-up, or to put on one of the Geisha wigs, but instead had piled her own russet locks high on top of her head and fixed them there with an ornate ivory comb.

Yasuko had prepared the main ingredients of the meal, leaving only the sweetmeats and later the tea, for the girl to offer.

It was obvious from the outset that she was treating the whole thing as a game, as an enormous joke to be laughed over in a few months time. She bowed to Greg before ever she spoke, and fluttered her fan too vigorously, and peeped over it with eyes which should have been coy, but which were only mocking. He thought she was genuinely shocked, genuinely contrite when he suddenly left the room and retired to bed.

The next evening was better; she was quieter and, although at first she said very little, when she did she spoke naturally, without candour or facetiousness. The chop—sticks finally broke the ice, Yasuko had been coaching her for days but she *still* hadn't got it right, and got in a terrible mess, and Greg moved to sit beside her and help her, and they laughed together. The conversation became easier now, especially after she heard of the ranch Greg had been brought up on, and the horses. They spoke endlessly of horses and riding and found that on that subject at least they had a great deal in common. Later she played for him. Technically she lacked finesse, but she had a good feeling for music, her touch was soft and Greg enjoyed it enormously. Later, when he stood up to leave she bowed to him, and there was no hint of mockery in it.

During the day she went riding. Greg had not only arranged to stable her own horse, but also bought five more and now they frequently went riding together. On these occasions she reverted to her jeans again, but Greg promised that he would send for a Samurai saddle and robes for her to try.

She played for him every evening now, and Greg noticed that Yasuko no longer arranged the flowers that sat either end of the low table, giving that responsibility instead to the girl. Her cooking had improved too, and she had mastered the chopsticks so that she now nimbly prepared and served this and that tit-bit for his enjoyment. He learned that she was a child of divorce, and had seen neither parent in some years, choosing to make her own way and serve an apprenticeship in London before opening her own hairdressers with the help of a bank loan, determination and a great deal of charm. When he once asked her why she had never married she had not replied, and he had not pressed the point, respecting her privacy as indeed she appeared to respect his.

After a while she took to bathing naked with Yasuko, and once with Semoi, but always, when Greg appeared she would reach for the towel by the side of the sunken bath and excuse herself. Somehow Greg was pleased that she did that and, in turn, he always took great care that she never came into the bath-house when he was there.

Later he was to wish that he had exercised the same care in the arena. She knew about Yoshi of course, there was no secret about that, but had always been out riding when they fought their mock battles.

One day however, some weeks after she had joined his household, he finished his fight against Yoshi and was bowing low when they were both startled to hear clapping and looked up to see her sitting in the gallery, Yoshi was more taken aback than he, he pulled off his mask and looked at her intently, and she at him.

The bath was a place for both men to relax together, it had nothing to do with cleanliness since each man had carefully washed his body from top to toe with hot towels before entering the bath. This time they did not relax, it was as though the girl, the intruder, hung between them. Yoshi was curious about her, as curious as politeness would allow, and Greg told him all about her. After that Yoshi lay back, his eyes closed, floating in the warm water.

Greg thought to reprimand her but then could think of no good reason why he should, and so did not even speak of it as they sat together at dinner that evening. For the first time she tried to question him about his love of things Oriental, about living here in England, but then, finding his answers evasive, she suddenly offered to massage him. She said that Yasuko had told her that certain Geishas were expert at such things, and if he cared for her to try? She wanted only to please him. He thanked her very gravely and formally, calling her 'Dianachan' in the Japanese manner, then explained that he was particularly tired and would go to bed early.

But he did not go to bed; he stood in his room before the mirror and gripped his aching shoulders and wondered why he had turned down her offer. Then he dressed himself again, left the house and drove to the club. He returned about an hour later, leaving the door ajar.

He began to notice a change in her behaviour, she was now always first, waiting for him at the table, and she sought his company more often during the day and sometimes, when he worked out against the sack of hardening cement slung from a tree, he would see her watching him from the house; he found himself consciously showing off, splitting hardwood planks with his feet, tiles with the flat of his hand. Oddly enough their conversations over dinner became less free, there were topics she would avoid, and once when he lightly questioned her about men friends, she actually blushed. He noticed too that on those occasions when he entered the bath house and she was there she no longer reached for her towel, but sat there with her shoulders showing out of the water and looked at him.

She had taken to wearing a Geisha wig too, and even attempted some brush work painting and he once came upon her experimentally binding her feet with bandages, but he forbade that and then tried to make a joke of it, but she did not smile.

They eventually settled into a topic of conversation that gave her no embarrassment and him a great deal of pleasure; for hours she would sit and gaze at him while he recounted tales of Ancient Japan, and of the customs and traditions that had been handed down, she was particularly interested in the history of the Geisha and asked many questions.

One day she shouted to him that she had mastered the Tea Ceremony, not to perfection of course, only one who had been sold as a child to the Geisha profession could ever have done that, but it was nicely, accurately done and pleased him very much indeed. She was quiet and soft eyed that evening, and yet he detected a tension about her, a fretfulness. Later he stood in his bedroom and thought about her. It was then that the door slid open behind him and she stood there, her kimono clasped loosely around her. "One hundred thousand pounds," she said, and let the kimono slip from her hands and settle like a flower around her feet and she was quite naked. Greg picked up the kimono and thrust it against her, she was bewildered, "Why?" she said, "Why?"

"We made a bargain," he replied. "And I am prepared to break the bargain," she pulled the kimono aside again, "I absolve you from it."

Greg shook his head, "No," he said softly, "No, Dianachan," She was close to tears now, "Why?" she said again, "Why!" and then ironically, "Because Japan is a long way away?" "A bargain is a bargain," said Greg, "But that is not the only reason. It would spoil things." He slowly slid the door closed upon her.

The next day she went out riding for hours, only galloping back to change one sweat lathered horse for another, and then off again, the slim whip flaying at her mount's flanks.

The day after that Yoshi came again. She was in the gallery even before they had begun, and Greg was annoyed to see that she had abandoned the wig, and even the Geisha hairstyle, and had let her long burnished hair fall about her shoulders, the kimono too was carelessly secured so that it fell open from the throat, to reveal the beginning swell of her breasts. She smiled a great deal, but at Yoshi most of the time.

Greg could never remember such a fight, he felt in tune, at a peak, and Yoshi's equal at last. But Yoshi was better than Greg thought possible, they fought six grim fights and Yoshi won them all. He did not speak to Greg during the fighting either, did not coach him.

Greg stood by a window and watched Yoshi climb into his car, but he did not immediately drive away because then the girl appeared and called to Yoshi. Greg could not hear what they said, but they stood and spoke to each other and smiled a great deal before Yoshi eventually drove away.

Yoshi came more frequently after that, he insisted that Greg needed all the training he could get, and Greg accepted that but each time, after the session was over, he would stand by the window and watch Yoshi and the girl talking to each other, and once they walked away towards the woods together.

Her formality at the dinner table was rigorous and quite perfect now; she would serve and tend to his needs and listen to his conversation with great attention, and happily join in on subjects of mutual interest, yet Greg thought that rather than coming closer together they seemed to be further apart than ever before.

He watched her as she played the harpsichord, her back and whole posture making a deliberate and complimentary curve from the instrument like a perfectly conceived painting, he watched her and thought again of how she had looked standing in the doorway of his room.

The last time Yoshi came to the house it was raining very hard so that when he entered the hallway water fell from his clothes and plastered his thick black hair flat against his forehead. The girl came laughing with a towel for him and began to dry his head and neck. And then his face, and Yoshi suddenly took her hands and held them still for a moment and looked at her. Then looked at Greg.

"A drink first," Yoshi had never asked for a drink before a bout, but Greg wasn't really surprised. They sat in Greg's study in silence, and Greg knew that Yoshi would speak soon, "She can be released from you by marriage," then standing up to give the words even greater import, "I wish to release her." Greg did not even bother to ask her feelings on the matter, that was not the way of things. "You are my friend," he said, "and a trusted visitor to my home."

Yoshi nodded, it was good that Greg had got straight to the point and saved Yoshi from further embarrassment, "I am indeed your friend, and you are mine, and this is an unhappy affair, but fortunately we are both men of honour."

They did not speak again until they stood in the arena and Greg had dismissed a surprised then anxious Semoi, and locked the door against the girl. Only then did he open the tall beechwood cupboard and take out the sheathed swords, that had been made before Columbus was born, but made by master craftsmen so that the blades still shone, were still supple, and still held an edge sharper than any razor.

Greg closed the cupboard door on the masks and armour, and they both stripped until they wore nothing but the loincloth, a roll of material wound around and under the genitals and then tucked into itself. Greg did not slip the scabbard into his loincloth but, like Yoshi, held it flat against the side of his body. They took up their positions, lightly bowed to each other, and then were ready to fight. Neither moved yet because the first move in such a fight would be like the first move in a game of chess— and for every move, particularly the first, there is always a counter.

They remained immobile for several minutes, only their eyes betraying any animation, eyes boring into eyes, each seeking the intentions of the other. It was Yoshi who moved at last, who moved first; Yoshi The Master, and perhaps it was this knowledge of omnipotence that gave him the confidence to move first. His sword flashed from the scabbard, rose behind his head and then came curving in with a sweeping horizontal stroke.

Greg countered; his stroke, coming as it did, straight from the scabbard end upwards, was more economical by a fraction, touching and diverting Yoshi's blade and then exultantly continuing so that the sharp edge of his sword sliced into Yoshi's body and up and across it in a blow of frightening power.

Yoshi stepped back and lowered his sword, then stepped back again until he was hard up against the wall and swaying slightly. He looked down at his body; Greg's cut had taken him from the groin, across his chest, and ended at his throat; one long, unbroken wound encompassing every vital organ in his body. It lay there for a moment, like a delicate pencil line, and then it began to bleed, very thinly because at no point had Greg's sword cut deeper than the skin itself, a scratch, a red stripe of defeat.

Yoshi ran his hand along the cut, and then looked at Greg, "I am dead," he said, and tossed his sword to the ground, "You will never see me again." He bowed, picked up his kimono and went to unlock the door.

The girl stood outside, with Yasuko and Semoi, their faces pale and frightened. Yoshi pushed between them and walked away, and for a moment the girl turned as though to pursue him, but then she didn't, and instead looked at Greg. "I shall miss Yoshi," he said, and left the arena.

He never knew if she waited for him at dinner that night, he stood at the bar of the club and drank as he had not drunk since the old carousing days with Bart, straight unwatered Scotch and many of them. Several girls attempted to speak to him but soon quietly edged away and left him alone.

As he drove back through the gateway he took a large slice off the spruce tree and the chrome trim off the Rolls. Semoi and Yasuko were waiting for him but he shouted at them fiercely, picked up a bottle of Japanese whisky and went to his bedroom. She was waiting for him there in the shadows, sitting on her suitcases and wearing jeans, a denim shirt, leather jacket, and that silly woollen hat. She was wearing her shoes too, and Greg immediately noticed where the wood floor was scratched and scuffed.

She stood up as he entered and perhaps, because the lanterns burned very low, did not see right away that he was drunk. She offered him a scrap of paper, but he did not move. "Take it" she said, "It's a cheque—you see—one hundred thousand pounds, the bargain is broken."

He still did not move, and now she came to him, "Don't you see," she said, "It's impossible. We can't go on like this. I can't go on," then, more softly, "I'm sorry," and she turned to pick up her suitcases.

"No" Greg spoke at last, "No, a bargain is a bargain." "I'm breaking it," she replied, and again thrust the cheque at him. He stared at it, then took it and tore it in two, "No." "I'm sorry" she said again, "But it just can't work. It never could."

His voice was surprisingly controlled and unslurred, "Three months notice, we have a contract, a legal contract." She stared at him, "You wouldn't hold me to that?" "Wouldn't I? I'll run you through the courts until your business, 'every penny you have is gone. A contract, a perfectly legal contract." He opened the bottle now and drank from it, and she did not move or speak for a long moment, but then she tugged the woollen cap off her head and shook her long hair loose, "Very well, three months from today, but you KNOW it isn't going to work, don't you?," Greg moved to flop onto the cushions of the bed, "It never does," he said, and leaned across to the lacquered cabinet beside his bed, slid open the drawer and took out the harikari sword, a short dagger with a wooden hilt that ran half its length and matching scabbard. Her curiosity was aroused now, "It NEVER does? You've been through all this before?"

"Not exactly" he replied, and then, "Please don't leave me, Dianachan, please." He rolled onto his side and whisky gurgled from the bottle.

She moved to take the bottle and right it, and saw that he was crying, she hesitated, then sat down beside him and put her hand against his cheek and was not sure what to do because he was such a powerful man to be crying like a baby. "Greg," she said softly, "Greg," and crouched low and cupped his face in her hands and kissed him. "Go away" he said, "Go away and leave me." "You'll really have to make up your mind," her voice was calmer now, more confident, "Don't leave you? Go away? Which am I to do?"

He turned, hands covering his face, fingers pressing against his eyes and then as she sat back, he took her hands and held them tightly. They looked at each other with a frankness that had never been between them before and, after a moment, she bent to kiss his face again and then suddenly he took her and held her very close. "Will you tell me now?" she said, "Will you tell me why?"

He told her then, at last, as she sat very still, he told her.

Told her about his father's ranch and how the ranges had been free and clear as far as the mountains until they found the oil that, had made them rich, the oil that scarred and blackened that wonderful country and spoiled it forever; then the terrible chain reaction, the riches from the oil being invested in other projects, foundries and factories built in other parts of the country and always spoiling and always making yet more money with which to despoil other places. The company growing bigger and more powerful and now seeking other countries to sack and pillage, until one day they looked towards the East, towards Japan. At first it had been merely a merger with a Japanese company already established in industrial Tokyo and Greg had gone there to administrate and had immediately fallen in love with the country. "At last I'd found somewhere with roots that went back not just a hundred years, but thousands! Mannered, ordered, formalised, everything, even where a farmer hung his sickle had meaning."

Gradually he became less American and more and more Japanese, adopting the dress, the language, the whole way of life, and taking for his own their history, *their* legends. He WAS Japanese. But the changes started to come there too, and his company as responsible as any; land being torn apart, the surgery of motor roads, but worse, the people themselves being eroded, "Not just the Coca-Cola culture, that was inevitable, but young men who no longer remembered the old ways, and when they did they laughed!"

Greg looked at her, "I had to leave, I couldn't go back to the States— that would have been like seeing a friend you remembered as young now old and dying. I chose Britain because they still respect a man's privacy here, his eccentricities, and they resist change, or they are slower to make it than most. I chose Britain because I knew I could not stay in Japan!" The girl frowned, "Could not?"

Greg picked up the small sword now, the harikari sword, shaped and honed on both edges for the ritual of disembowellment, "I am Japanese, in my soul I am Japanese, and that is irrevocable, that is fatal," he looked at her, "They—we—are a fatalistic race you know. To die in battle is the ultimate accolade, but the next best thing is to die properly by one's own hand." She stared at him with a growing comprehension now, and he nodded, "Yes, if I had stayed in Japan I know, I absolutely *know*, what I would have eventually done. What I would have had to do." She took the sword from him and slid hilt from scabbard a fraction to reveal an inch or two of bright steel, "You still haven't explained about us."

"Don't you see" he said, "The relationship between a man and his Geisha is perfect, it is all joy, and nobody, NOBODY can spoil that."

She put her hand under his chin and lifted it, "But the relationship between a man and a woman can be perfect too."

He watched her as she slowly and carefully removed her jacket, and then unbuttoned her shirt from throat to waist and proudly pulled it wide. He did not move, "Dianachan," he whispered, "Dianachan, what if?," she put her finger to his lips, silencing him, and then she took up the sword, drew it from its scabbard and put the point to her own belly and pushed it into her flesh, "In that case," she said, "We will do it together, when the time comes."

He took her then, gently then with an increasing animal hunger, and they made love.

Later he slept and she stood by the window with his kimono draped around her and she knew that tomorrow he would release her from the contract in the way that Yoshi had sought to release her. Although she was happier than she could ever remember she cried, and then smiled quizzically as she wondered why he had never noticed, or how long it would take him to notice her wrists, and the thin, jagged, long-healed razor scars.

RABBIT PIE

I DIDN'T SEEK HIM OUT, THAT'S NOT MY WAY, BUT clearly sooner or later, he was going to seek me out, if I stayed in the pub long enough.

Notting Hill is now what the politicians call an 'ethnic area', and of course the pubs reflect this. Like this one I was in now, just along the road from the police station, he and I the only white faces to be seen; and that included the barmen.

So he would be bound to seek me out sooner or later, because he needed to talk, or at least be with someone. If you ask me how I knew that, I would have to reply that it's a knack I have; I study people, and I know. That's how I knew about him; a thick-set, powerful man with a day's stubble on his chin and a grubby old coat that might have been slept in. But that just told me he was careless about his appearance and had perhaps been working late. The hands were the real giveaway; strong hands, and yet pudgy in repose, the knuckles were a white line where he gripped the bar so tightly, and had been for the last five minutes. A man under stress with something terrible suppressed inside of him. His eyes had that pale liquid look of a man who has drunk too much. Not that he was at all drunk; he had gulped down four large Scotches in the past ten minutes, and looked good for a whole lot more. He was clenching his jaw too; the pub was noisy but the sharp little sound of his teeth carried through. Yes, he would have to talk sooner or later.

He ordered another drink, then caught a glimpse of me in the mirror for the first time—which surprised me because I'd have thought he was a man who would always know what was going on around him. He took his drink, then hesitated, then came away from the bar and sat down at my table. "Do you mind?" he muttered. I shook my head, after all I'd been expecting it.

He didn't speak again until he had finished his drink, then stood up again, looked at my half empty glass and said, "Hate drinking alone. Would you . . . ?" I'd be glad to. He nodded, went off and got our drinks and came back again. We said 'cheers' and sat in silence. Then he glanced around the bar and said, "I've got nothing against blacks," I waited, "Some say they should go back to the jungle—well, they wouldn't have to go bloody far, would they?" He pulled a crumpled paper from his pocket, laid it on the table, and tapped it, "Did you see this?" His thick, grubby fingernail indicated a story about a young girl who had been killed in a hit and run accident. Yes, as a matter of fact, I was aware of it.

"Murder" he said, "Murder," and then, realising he might have said too much, "Don't mind me. Been drinking all day." I took this opportunity of offering another round of drinks, and went over to get them. He just sat and stared into his empty glass, not even looking up when I returned, or when he asked me which political party I voted for. My answer, that I found them all much of a muchness and therefore did not vote for any seemed to satisfy him, "You're wise," he said, "And as for this mob that's in power now . . . !" I took this as my cue to dig a little deeper.

He was evasive at first and, despite all the drink, still very cautious; he turned the conversation around to me, asked me who I was, what I did. My answers must have satisfied him because, another drink later, he told me his name, and what he did for a living. A policeman; a Detective Sergeant, "From the station just along the road."

I retorted with the usual guess that he must have seen some strange things in his time.

That's when the glass surrendered to those white knuckles and broke in his hand. Luckily he wasn't cut, but *this* time, as I renewed the drinks, I set up three for each of us. I had a feeling he was about to tell me all about it. And I was right.

"It was just last evening, I was about to go off duty and go home when we got this call. From a Pakistani who lived about a mile away, in one of those big old houses, Victorian, split into more then a dozen rooms and flats. The house was known to us, we'd had a bit of trouble there from time to time. It's cheap you see, and a kind of jumping off point for families, some of them quite respectable, before they find something better. But it's also a place prostitutes use to take their customers. Yes, we'd had a bit of trouble there before. Well this man you see, told us that his daughter had noticed a stain on their ceiling, a dark sticky stain that was spreading, and looked like blood!

"We didn't take it too seriously, one of the boys said probably someone upstairs had 'over-turned his curry bowl'. Anyway, I had to pass right by the place on my way home, so I agreed to check it out.

"Well, I've been on this job for a few years, I've seen plenty of violent crime, I've seen blood, and as soon as I saw that ceiling I knew he was right, it *was* blood! He couldn't tell me who had the room above, it was one of those let out on an hourly basis.

"So I crept up the stairs and listened at the door. I could hear *something*, movement, breathing, I wasn't sure. Now in cases like this where a crime of violence is suspected the rules of entry don't apply. I stepped back as far as the landing would allow and measured up that door; breaking a door down may look easy on television, but it isn't. That single kick at the lock routine? If they have a good bolt secured all you end up with is a sprained ankle, or worse. I hit it with my shoulder and I was lucky because the woodwork was as rotten as the rest of the building. I burst into that stinking, grim little room and they both looked at me with startled faces, the girl and the man, but I barely noticed her, just the man, that man. I recognised him immediately."

He stopped now and drank the second of the three drinks I had set up for him. I wondered if he would tell me the name, or merely refer to him, as policemen sometimes do, as 'Mister X'. That was important. Or would he think better of it and merely conclude the story at this tantalising point? He gnawed on a thumbnail for a moment or two and then spat out the name, yes, *spat* it out with a venom that was frightening to see and hear. It was the name of a man I would immediately recognise too, anyone would. The name of a man who at this moment occupies a high Ministerial post within the Government, and who many freely believe may well become Prime Minister one day.

"They were both naked of course, him and the girl, and they were doing . . . well I'd rather not tell you what they were doing . . . I've got a kid of my own about that age. She was just fifteen, you see, under age. Fifteen, and you can't really blame them when they're that young can you? No, you have to blame the man. It was disgusting."

He picked up the third drink, stared at it, and then put it down again and looked at me.

"You're wondering about the blood? Well, I haven't told you the worst of it. Him and the girl, that was bad enough but somehow where sex is concerned even if you can't forgive everything, you can understand, just. It was the rabbits."

Rabbits! This was something even I had not been prepared for. Rabbits? He nodded, "There were twelve of them, a round dozen. The bed was one of those old brass frame affairs with bars, and from every bar he'd hung a rabbit, tied 'em by their back legs and hung 'em. Most of them were dead by then, but there were a couple still alive, still jerking. He'd cut their throats you see, and watched them die, poor things, watched them bleed to death while he and the girl did . . . *that*. To add to the excitement . . . I suppose."

He fell silent again, then sipped at his third drink and braced himself for the final foray. "I didn't hit him. Wanted to but even I knew that it wasn't on hitting a Minister of the Crown . . . ! I called the station from the phone on the landing outside. When I went back into the room some of the shock had left him and now, with his clothes back on again, some of that old banter and bluster that you see in the news reels had come back. He seemed sure of himself again—confident. The girl was crying now.

"We didn't speak at all while we waited, we just stood there in that room, him lighting a cigarette now and the girl quietly crying, and those rabbits hanging there with their throats cut.

"The car was a long time coming and when it did arrive there were none of the usual boys, they were faces I didn't know and the officer in charge was a full Superintendent from a West End Division. They'd brought a blanket; to put over his head when they lead him away. There was no blanket for the girl though, she was taken away by a police woman in a different car. I said, 'what about the rabbits—what are we going to do with them?', and the Superintendant smiled and said, 'Probably make them into a pie!'"

He stared into his now empty glass, the knuckles were no longer white but he was not a man who had relaxed, but a man who was spent, resigned.

"When I got back to the station I started out to make my report then was told it wasn't necessary, it would all be handled at the West End Division, I protested that—I was the arresting officer . . . ! That's when the chief sent for me. I'll say something for the old boy, I think he was angrier than I was, 'The pack's been called off,' those were his very words, 'The pack's been called off,' and I was to take a week's leave and forget the incident ever happened, and never talk of it again. A white wash! Well, I'd heard of such things happening, but never really believed it was possible. It was possible. It is possible. But it doesn't stop there."

He tapped the newspaper that lay between us, tapped the story of the young girl killed in the hit and run, "That was her," he said, then suddenly he stood up and without a word, without a gesture, walked out of the pub.

I stood up too, paused for a moment to look at that newspaper again, with just a touch of regret now, and then I followed him out.

He was some yards away walking hunched and slowly, I got into my car and started the engine, there were other people in the street but it didn't matter because the number plates were false. Nevertheless it would be much easier than the young girl, she had contacted a National newspaper and the whole assignment had been tinged with panic, I had had to run her down in daylight, on a broad and busy thoroughfare.

I set the car moving and stalked him down the street judging my speed to a nice perfection so that we should meet on the corner, just at the moment he began to cross. His foot left the kerb and mine plunged the accelerator; he must have known it was me, for a brief moment our faces were close, a foot or two apart at most, his eyes staring into mine. Then I swung the wheel, controlled the skid and he was gone, just a frozen figure in my mirror shocked into immobility by the edge of the kerb, shocked into sobriety. He would know now. He would be more careful, and he really ought to be more careful.

They hadn't told me about the rabbits. It was the one element they had omitted, and I like rabbits. As a matter of fact I keep half a dozen as pets, a blue, several Angoras and a silky Caucassian. Yes, I like rabbits very much indeed.

I drove into the city. I needed to find a pub. A busy pub, somewhere I could have a few drinks, and find someone to talk to.

IRISH JOKE

RILEY PURSED HIS LIPS AND LOOKED AT MALLEY
and Casey and Sean and thought, well, there's one thing for it,
when the whole damned thing is over one day at least we'll be spared a
new batch of rousing or sentimental ballads with endless verses; I mean,
you can hardly sing bravely of shaving the heads of young girls, or taking
the legs and arms off helpless people. And there was nothing pretty to
rhyme with kneecaps.

Not that Riley wanted the whole damned thing over too quickly, oh,
no. But then Riley was different from the rest; like Malley now, fired with
a patriotism and dream of a united Ireland, and a hatred of the English
that reached back to the Great Famine of two hundred years before. Or
Casey, self styled 'Captain' Casey who had reasoned it out in a political
way and loved to fight (or at least give orders) and if he weren't fighting
this battle would be off no doubt, to some other trouble spot where a man
of limited talent but a great deal of tenacity could quickly make himself
infamous and see his own face beaming out of a few newspapers. And
Sean, who was very young and slightly stupid and, for the first time in his
life, and perhaps the only time, felt important. Riley's cause was made of
stronger stuff, 'Riley's cause was Riley and he did it purely and only for the
money, crisp green American dollars that came smuggled in from New
York and Boston Irishmen who had never seen Ireland in their whole
lives; and some of it too, Riley suspected, from the coffers of the arms
dealers who were only making a sensible businesslike investment.

Riley was a genuine explosives expert and much sought after because although there were other bombmen they were amateur, and did not always know what they were doing, especially with the sometimes unstable stuff they had to work with, and there had been frequent fiascos, bombs that didn't explode, and worse, bombs that did . . . while they were still, in the bombmaker's hands!

Riley's bombs always exploded where and when they were meant, and always on time. This one was set for twelve noon. Malley had wanted to go for ten minutes after one on the theory that most of the offices emptied for lunch after one, and many of the girls and other workers would go window shopping around the store and it would be at its most crowded then. Riley had dissuaded him, not out of humani-tarian reasons but out of experience, pride in his craft. He pointed out that sometimes too big a crowd could nullify the effects of a bomb, a human barrier containing the explosion much as sandbags might, no, the store should be crowded, but not too crowded then the effects might reach . . . well . . . to the mezzanine as well. So they settled for twelve noon.

It was a very handy bomb, the best so far Riley admitted to himself. It was safe too because they had got hold of some of the marvellous, inert until detonated 'plastique'; that was the heart of the device, the plas-tique and its detonator, linked to a tiny, cell operated alarm clock, about half the size of a matchbox. This was Riley's master-stroke because it not only reduced the size dramatically but, with the aid of a equally tiny booster he was able to use the cell of the clock to activate the detonator. Around it all he constructed a cage. Six inch nails, nicked here and there so that they would fragment, and laid end to end and lightly soldered together into a box-like framework. Then around this he built the second cage, this, as he put it together, reminded him of the delicately fragile fretted work he had seen in mosques in Saudia Arabia (Before they threw him out for making his own still); it was constructed of smaller, much thinner nails each dipped and tipped with lead to give them the lethal velocity required to shatter flesh and bone. Riley was very proud of it. The whole thing exactly fitted into a card-board carton which, on the outside, announced that it held four pairs of sheer tights, in caramel. That had been Casey's contribution, he had investigated the store two weeks ago and had been struck by the lingerie department on the ground floor; at the end of each counter was a waste basket, and every basket contained a number of similar boxes—but they were empty.

It was quite heavy, but Sean had practiced carrying it deep in the inside poacher's pocket of his raincoat, carrying it with his hand lightly against his side, slightly lifting the box and supporting it. All he had to do now was to stroll near a lingerie counter, drop his box amongst the others in the waste basket, and leave. Before twelve noon of course.

Sean was to plant the bomb because it was a chance to become a hero in his own time and earn the plaudits and lasting respect of his fellow countrymen. At least that's what they told him. The real reason was that, in the past, bomber's had been noticed and identified later, or had been caught in one of the occasional spot checks made at every store from time to time and had ended up in prison for practically the rest of their lives, and neither Malley or Casey wanted that, and Riley—even if he had agreed to do it (which he wouldn't)—was much too valuable to risk on such a mundane task.

Nevertheless they tried to minimise all risk; there would be no stolen car to be noticed and picked up by some over zealous copper. Sean hired the car legitimately, using his own name and driving licence, and had already picked the spot where he would park it for a few minutes, just across from the store and, admittedly on a no parking yellow line, but that was an offence the most law abiding were often guilty of . . .

He left the sleazy room at eleven o'clock and drove off, they watched him drive off, and then Malley opened the bottle of Jameson's, but Casey looked at him warningly—it was too soon for celebration, so Malley put the bottle down again, but Riley drank from it.

In the early days they would have been packed and on their way home by now, but experience had shown that departures just before or after a bombing brought more than keen interest from the Special Branch, and your name and face in a file for evermore. So these days they sat tight, hoping the address they had chosen was cover enough, and often waking in the night sweating, and reaching under the bed for the pump shotgun.

Casey had timed the route three times and, making allowances for the vagaries of traffic, they knew when to expect Sean back—just before twelve. The next hour or so did not pass quickly, save for Riley, who now lay on the bed and swigged from the bottle.

When Sean was one minute behind the latest scheduled time Malley began to fidget, two minutes and then the panic set in, he spun round to Riley and said "Get your bags." But then Casey, who was still at the window said, "No, here he comes." Malley rushed to the window to confirm with his own eyes, and indeed there was Sean just parking the car, and now moving towards the house. Malley moved away towards the door but Casey remained at the window, "Nobody following," he said.

Malley opened the door and practically pulled the boy into the room; he stood there, pale and trembling slightly. But that was O.K., that was to be expected, "Well?" demanded Malley, Sean just stared at him. "Give the lad a chance" said Casey, "He knows the proper way to report." But Malley gripped Sean's shoulders, "Are we all right? Did you do it? Did you get away with it?" Sean's face cleared now, he nodded, "Oh, yes, I got away with it."

Malley turned, beaming now at Casey then moving across to take the whisky, bottle from Riley, and wipe the top of it, with the flat of his hand, but then Casey took the bottle from him before he could drink, and Malley looked as though he might protest, but then nodded as Casey handed the bottle to Sean. He swigged and coughed, and touched his forehead with his hand as though the drink had reached him quickly.

"We should hear the bang from here," Riley sat up now, swung his feet to the floor and glanced at his watch, "About a minute."

Sean did not remove his coat, but sat down and again held his head, Casey regarded him proudly, "You did well, lad, struck a blow," then hesitated. "You were a little bit late back."

Sean nodded and, "I had an accident."

Malley choked on the bottle, "An accident? What do you mean?"

"It might have been worse," Sean replied, "I was sitting at the lights and some fool of a learner driver in front of me. Put the damned thing into reverse and came back into me. I hit my head on the windscreen," he again rubbed his forehead and they could see now a dark bruise beginning to show just under the hairline.

"Were the police involved?" asked Malley.

"Yes" replied Sean, "copper standing across the street."

The panic of before edged back again now, "And what did you say, lad? What did he ask?" Casey spoke gently because he knew the boy to be slow witted at the best of times.

"I said I was all right, didn't want to make a complaint. I didn't even have to give him my name or licence," he looked at them with a touch of defiance now, "I TOLD you I got away with it."

Casey met Malley's eyes and a nod passed between them, "We're all right then," said Malley, "All right."

But Riley came and stood over the boy and looked at that bruise and that pale face, looked into the clouded eyes, "Was this before or after you planted the bomb?" he asked.

Sean stared at him, "Bomb?" he echoed, and then something in his face started to clear, and he stood up now and thrust his hand into his raincoat pocket and produced a box that should have contained four pairs of sheer tights. In caramel.

The silence in the room was such that Riley could hear his own watch ticking, and then, faintly, from far off, a church clock starting to strike twelve. Riley's bombs always exploded on time.

DON'T LOOK

YOU MUST HAVE HEARD THAT STORY, YOU MUST have. It's been around for years and, like a classic joke, has passed around the world and back again. Usually, to give it greater impact, the teller tells it in the first person, as though it happened to him.

It's about being on the London tube (or the Subway if it's being told in New York, or a train almost anywhere in the world), and you, the story-teller, sitting there, travelling home late at night. There are just two other people in the compartment; an anonymous man on your side but further up, and the man sitting opposite. You are intrigued by the man, then worried, because he is staring with such a fixed expression, and he looks so pale; you sit there wondering if you should get involved, whether you should lean forward, tap him on the knee and ask if he is all right. Then someone taps you, on the shoulder, it is the anonymous man, and his face is very grave as he hands you a scrap of paper then moves to resume his seat.

You look at the scrap of paper, and it says, "The man opposite you is dead, get out at the next station and do not look back."

Well, that's it, that's the story, sort of shaggy dog because there is no real conclusion to it. You must have heard, perhaps even told it. One of those apocryphal stories handed from mouth to mouth. Except that it isn't apocryphal, you see, I'm the man it really happened to.

111

I DID get out at the next station, don't ask me to reason why, perhaps it was the sheer urgent authority in the face of the anonymous man. So I got out, then as the tube train—it was the tube, and it was London—prepared to pull out again, and the doors made that little hiss before closing, I jumped back on again, in the next compartment.

I waited a moment, then crept along the swaying carriage until I came to the glass door with a view through to the compartment I had just vacated. He was still there, the pale, staring man, but there was no sign of the anonymous man.

Then suddenly the train must have crossed points or something, the lights flickered and dimmed, then went out altogether for a few moments; I felt a sharp blow in the centre of my back and then the sensation of falling, falling.

I don't remember opening my eyes again, I think they must have been wide open when I came round. I was seated now and felt very stiff, I wanted to stand up, stretch my limbs, but I couldn't move, not my legs, arms, nothing. Not even my eyes. Across from me sat a young couple, a girl and a boy, they were laughing and talking, I could hear the murmur of their voices, and then the girl looked at me, then turned to whisper to the boy, and they both looked at me. There was concern in their faces and yet hesitation too. I thought for a moment that the girl was about to stand up, but then someone else entered my field of vision, he was a familiar face, the anonymous man, he bent briefly and momentarily obscured the boy and girl from my sight, but then he moved away again, and I saw that they were both staring at a scrap of paper the girl held, and then at me.

The train ran to a stop now, and they both hastily got up and moved away, I tried to move my eyes in appeal, tried to scream after them, but my larynx was paralysed. I just sat there, and felt the motion of the train as it moved on again.

Then the anonymous man reappeared before me again, but he wasn't looking at me, but back towards the next compartment. He sighed and slid a hypodermic out of his pocket. He spoke then, but really to himself, "Silly fools, silly young fools," he turned and caught my fixed stare mutely seeking explanation, "It's a little game I play," he explained, "I call it 'Lot's Wife'," then moved away, presumably to the next carriage.

KNOCKER

WHEN GEORGE MALLEY BREEZED INTO A PUB WHERE he was not known most took him to be connected with racing. A tall, powerful, red-faced man with meaty fists and wrists to match, he rarely wore anything save tweeds or checks, and always a jaunty cap. 'Racing'. Definitely. Wise heads would nod. Probably a trainer. The touch of Irish brogue helped reinforce an impression that George took care never to dispel. Actually, although it is true to say that he did enjoy the occasional flutter on the horses, George was a knocker. Not a difficult term to run down because it described exactly what George did for his lucrative living. He knocked on doors. Or was it, as George sometimes wondered, because he knocked people down, way down, in price?

No one knew better than George that knocking was a craft, a fine art even. To knock on the door of a complete stranger and then persuade him or her to part with a potentially valuable antique—even if she or he thought it to be only junk—that took some doing. And George had been doing it for some tune, as his bank manager would testify.

He had started with a horse-drawn cart, ten pounds in cash (they always seemed to be a bit bedazzled by actual folding cash) and a box of balloons for the kids—balloons that had been rejected by even the cheapest cracker factories and would last about as long as it took George to move on to the next house.

George had a Volvo estate car now, and a Rolls, and a mistress tucked away in Bath. In between the horse and cart and the mistress a lot of water had passed under the bridge for George; although on certain days, when some of that water, along with a Glenfiddich, was just reaching his kidneys, he'd look at his mistress and think, 'That was a bloody good horse and cart'. Been through it all had George. Acquired a lot of experience. Time was when he thought a 'commode' meant only one thing, but times change, and now many of the big London dealers—and the Germans, and the Belgians—sought George out. They came and knocked at *his* door, because George knew how to turn up a fine piece.

Knew all the tricks did George, and once upon a time he carried a dart in his pocket to stab the underside of tables with and then display, 'riddled with worm', to some hapless owner. "Goes like wildfire," George would continue, spreading alarm and despondency like a rare plague, "You'll be well rid of this. I'll take it off your hands."

And most times, he did. In those days he even 'carried the coin' the coin to be dropped and spun to the far end of a long dark hallway when he'd got just one toe in the door and had spied something tasty at the far end. "Excuse me—dropped some money . . . don't mind, do you?" He used to work with a 'ferret' too, a partner, preferably small and nimble, someone who would scuttle away to 'case' the place while George engaged the fuddled owners in conversation. He worked alone these days—after all, a partner meant splitting the profits. Yes, George preferred to work alone now.

His technique had changed too. Television was partly responsible for that; all those programmes telling the uninitiated just how valuable the contents of their attic might be. George had three televisions, but no licence.

Some knockers are jealous about their working methods, but not George; he boasted of it—because it couldn't be pinched. Not unless you were another George. He broke it down into two parts. The first part was 'intimidation'—after all, these days, if someone as big and prepossessing as George turned up at your door, you were so damned glad to find out that he didn't intend to mug you that the battle was half won! George *did* mug them—but they didn't know at the time. The second part of his technique, which would cost you at least three large Scotches to find out—or a bottle of Beaune '56 (the horse and cart wasn't the only thing George had left behind him)—was purely his own invention: 'selection'—of the weakest, of those most likely to succumb to his over bearing manner. Yes, working on the premis of 'It's easier to kick a man who's already halfway down', George specialised in terrorising bargains out of the infirm and the aged. His greatest achievement, his 'cup de grass' as he would call it (George hadn't come that far from the horse and cart!) had been "This old boy in an iron lung. Looking at the room through a mirror. So when I pick up this lovely lump of old Chelsea—*and he insists it is*—I show him the mark, don't I? And in the mirror it's back to front, isn't it? So it's a steal from him for £5. *Five quid—an absolute steel.*" That was always worth at least another Scotch—out of someone else's pocket—because George never believed in buying his own drinks.

George felt good today, felt the promise of something big around the next corner, or the next. The promise? No, more a need, because the last couple of weeks had been mediocre, they hadn't stretched George's infinite talents. Of course there had been the six Windsor chairs but the old dear had been practically blind, and half simple too. He hadn't even had to slip out his bit of sandpaper to rough up the tops of the chairs for her to feel 'how far gone' they were. No, profitable as it had been—six quid to the old biddy, six hundred from the dealer—it didn't really count.

George needed a steal, a fillip, a story for the pub—and the guarantee of free drinks for most of the evening. He turned the wheel of his brand new Volvo estate and reflected that there were some who deliberately hid the posh motor, dressed down, affected poverty so as to allay the suspicions of their victims—but not George. He adjusted the knot of his Jermyn Street tie tighter to his Harvey and Hudson shirt, and shrugged the shoulders of his Harry Hall hacking jacket. Not George! Part of the challenge, part of the excitement, was to let them know that they were dealing with the very best—game of wits, with the dice always loaded in George's direction. So temporarily preoccupied was he that he almost drove right past the cottage. Earlier on at the local pub he had invested a half a pint into one of the locals and learned that an old couple lived down the lane. An old couple who had seen better days. George smelt blood.

He stopped right outside the cottage. 'If they're watching, let them! Let them wonder. Let them start to get a bit scared . . . Property developer perhaps, come to look at the place before I pull it down around their ears? Or a plain-clothes policeman'—George has sometimes been mistaken for that 'nosing around?' Either way they are already nervous, off balance.

He might have made a good policeman because he immediately noticed pertinent things; the garden for instance, a profusion of those purple and red flowers that grow close to the ground and are beloved of old ladies—but uncared for, getting overgrown. "Getting frail, and they can't afford a gardener," thought George. And the curtains—good quality chintz but now long faded and in need of replacement. But most of all, the woodpile—rotting logs and twigs gleaned from nearby fields, but amongst them some old pieces of broken timber: a broken carved oak panel, a piece of a drawer still wearing a nice and original Regency escutcheon for the lock. Alarm prickled at George's neck, "Dear God, I hope they haven't chopped all the good pieces up!"

He knocked on the door with his bare knuckles. Even though there was a bell pull hanging nearby, he knocked. One of the traditions of the trade.

Georges assessment had been correct; the little old man who opened the door was frail and shabby. "My goodness, dad, you look terrible." Hit 'em first and hit 'em hard. "Few days by the sea would do you good." And then the offer of hope "Perhaps I can make it possible for you." He stepped past and around the old man and entered the hallway. "Shabby place," he meant it, there wasn't an item in sight, "Down on your luck, eh? Yes, I sympathise with folks like you, making do on a pittance of a pension. That's why I try to help 'em out."

The old man was still wheezing, gathering his breath preparatory to speech. George moved further down the hall, opening a door to peep into the front room—a vase there. Maybe. A couple of chairs. No rich seam yet.'

"Who is it, dear?" The old lady—the wife—was an absolute gift to George, faded, shaky on her feet, and yet the eyes sharp and clever. Yes, she thought she still knew it all. George instinctively knew that any bargaining would be done with her.'

"Lovely to meet you, ma'am," the courtly manners suddenly putting the old man between anger and curiosity, "Lovely." George bent to pick up the frail fingers and lightly kiss them—at the same time quickly establishing the quality of any rings there. Nothing. The usual plain, very worn gold band, and an amethyst that wouldn't fill a fly's codpiece.

He gazed again into those sharp, clear eyes. "Oh, but he's not looking after you properly, is he?" Divide and conquer. "No, a breath of sea air is what you want."

The old man had stopped wheezing and now his mouth fully opened to speak. George forestalled him yet again. "I know, I know, you can't afford it. Same old story these days. Well, I'm going to do my very best to help you afford it. Just take a look upstairs." He was up the staircase two at a time, knowing he would be on his way down again before the old man even made halfway.

And indeed he was. A couple of floaters—jugs and basins, wash-stand stuff—that he might chance a few pence on, and sell for around £40 each.

"Please?" the old lady managed to say before George was off again.

"Kitchen this way?"

The two old people stood askance in their hallway, much as they might have if a typhoon had blown through the house. George was back immediately. Four pieces of pink lustre and a teapot that looked like Rockingham, but wasn't. Never mind, that German dealer wasn't that clever, was he? Yes, it might be just up his jolly old Strasse. But hardly a big day for George. Outlay of—what—twenty quid at the most? And a return of no more than two hundred? Not George's usual profit margin.

"What do you want?" Having said this, the old man returned to his wheezing.

"What do I want!" Indignation.

"Yes," the old lady pursued, "We *could* call the police you know."

* "How?" replied George, "how do you know I'm not the police?"

They stood looking up at his big frame, his rosy face that could, in repose, assume an angry look. "You're *not* the police, are you?" asked the old lady.

George frowned at her. "Lot of stolen property around these days."

For a moment he thought the old lady might faint, and that he had pushed too far, but then she said, "There's nothing stolen here. All you see here has been in my family for years. Years."

"Has it now?" Georges interest quickened. "Well, about due to get rid of it, aren't you? And get yourself some new stuff?"

The old couple exchanged a glance. The old man controlled his wheezing again. "I see. You're one of those chaps who goes buying door to door."

George favoured them with his ever-so-friendly, to-be trusted smile at last. "I'm not one of those chaps, dad. I'm the one. Honest George Malley, and I'm out to do you a favour." His glance embraced the old woman too. "Both·of you. There's a chance, you see, that I might find something I could show you a handsome profit on—enough to take yourself to the seaside for a few days. And if you do . . . " He dug into his pocket and proffered them the card.

They stared at it as primeval man must have stared at the wheel. Then finally, "Patrick Mahon?" said the old man.

"Friend of mine," replied George, "And he'll be a friend of yours too. Runs the nicest little hotel you could hope to find—right on the sea front. Tell him you know me, and he'll give you a reduction." Obligation. And anyway George got a 10 percent kickback from Patrick for anyone he sent down to his sad little fleabag by—not the sea exactly, but the estuary.

While they were still bemused by his magnanimity, George opened the last door, opened it on to the tiny dining room. And there it was.

"There's always one piece," George often said, "Any household where the owners are more than seventy, you'll always find one piece worth the trouble." George had found his.

A walnut bureau, inlaid with holly and ebony, with pediment mountings, and made unusual, 'rare' thought George, by the fact that it had only two deep drawers. George moved towards it like Adam towards Eve during a sudden autumn, but the old man, quite surprisingly nimble for a few brief seconds, got there first and leaned against it, against the left hand drawer.

"It's not for sale," said the old man. Nevertheless George pulled out the right-hand drawer enough to see the exquisite dovetailing, and the rough saw marks of hand-cutting. He ran a hand along the front of the drawer and sensed the patina that only years can bring. This drawer belonged to a perfect 'right' piece and, while making that assessment, George also put a price on it—it had to be in excess of £3,000.

"This is a nice piece," he said. Shining honesty. "Very nice indeed."

"It was my great-grandmother's," blurted the old lady.

"Now, dear," the old man started to say, but she cut across his mild protest.

"No we must be as honest as he is," Turning those clear eyes on

George, she continued, "My great-grandmother. And I believe it was *given* to her. So it must be at least 180 years old."

George smiled. "Well, I hardly think as old as that, but old enough certainly." He turned his back on it now, and would never look at it again until it rested on top of his Volvo estate. Excite them. Get them on the hook. Then play them.

"I saw a jug and basin upstairs. Not special, but I'll give you £40 for it." About what it was worth on the really open market' but a sprat to catch a mackerel. Hold out the olive leaf of fair dealing, gain their confidence and then . . . the bureau.

The old man stared and George knew he hadn't actually *seen* forty pounds in a long time. George now casually produced his roll of notes; they filled his big, ample fist.

"Well . . . ?" The old man's eyes found his wife.

"It belonged to Alice," she snapped, "I never liked Alice."

The deal was agreed, and now George wandered about the house, buying this and that; some lace, a few spoons—even the teapot that could have been Rockingham but wasn't, at way, way above its value.

Lose the small ones to win the big one.

George carefully piled his purchases up in the hallway and then, finally, he turned and regarded them. "Now what about that old side board in there?"

"It's a bureau." said the old lady, "They call it a bureau." Bloody television!

"Whatever you call it. What about it? Can we do a deal?"

They hesitated. George rustled the notes he still held, because so far no money had changed hands. The mongoose never watched the snake any more intently than the old couple watched the money in George's hand.

He played his ace. "Because if we can't do a deal," he looked down at the pile of bric-a-brac on the floor, "it's hardly worth my while getting involved at all. You see. this stuff won't pay for my time and petrol." Sadly resigned. "No. with that cupboard at the right price I might just about break even, but without it . . . ?" He shook his head. He put the money away into his pocket again. "I'm sorry."

The old man packed up the jug. "But surely . . . ?"

George shook his head. "I'm sorry, dad. I got carried away, I suppose because I thought, when you saw I really meant business, you'd do me a price on that old thing in there."

"It's a bureau." George met her eyes. Yes, he had known from the start that she would be the one to beat.

"Seaside's very nice of this time of the year. And you both look as though you could do with it." He looked from one to the other. "You owe it to each other."

The old man hesitated, then said, "There's a lot gone into that bureau . . . "

Again the old lady interrupted him. "It belonged to my great-grand-mother, and *if* we were to sell it . . . "

"Yes," said George.

"If we were to sell it," she continued, "I would feel just awful about it." .

This was a new line of defence for George. He took a new tack. "Look at it this way, the thing's falling to pieces . . . probably got the worm in it too."

"No," said the old man. "that timber was all specially selected. There is no worm."

George got sidetracked then because it turned out that the old man had once worked for some cabinet makers and knew a thing or two about wood and carpentry and such things. George listened to the boring saga for a few minutes and then brought things back to his side of the fence. "Well, my mind is made up. Either I take all this junk and the bureau, or nothing."

The old couple looked as though they would have liked to go off to chat about it privately, but George wasn't giving them the chance. Having given them his whole repertoire from bombast to charm, he now came back to square one. "You've wasted enough of my time." He had opened the door, even got one foot across the doorstep, when the old lady spoke. "I would feel just awful about it." George turned back, waiting for the 'but'. "But if I used the money, to go and visit her grave . . . "

George smiled inside. 'That's more like it, where is she buried?'

"America."

It wasn't often that George found himself utterly off balance. "America?!"

"The West Coast, just outside San Francisco."

George stared at her. "Couldn't you just send some flowers?"

"We would have to visit," she insisted, "or I would not rest easy in my mind."

"America?! Both of you?"

The old man smiled. "You yourself said we deserved a break together."

Georges mind was spinning. "But America. The two of you. That would cost . . . "

"Six hundred and thirty six pounds." She glanced at her husband. "We were discussing it just the other day, weren't we?"

"Six hundred and thirty six . . . !"

"And with the other stuff you've bought—let's say a round seven hundred and fifty."

George actually stammered. "But . . . but . . . "

"I know it is really a bit more than that, but, well, you have been so nice with us."

It wasn't quite the story he had hoped to tell in the pub, but the bureau was worth at least ten times as much and . . . George looked at the old lady and knew the impasse had been reached. She didn't look so frail as she had, but rather—inflexible.

They helped George to load the bureau on to the rack on top of his estate car, even insisting on finding an old blanket to wrap around it, and then, as he finally drove away, the old man remained outside looking at the pile of old timbers. He rummaged through them, pulled out the drawer front and ran his hand over the Regency escutcheon. Like his own hand it had the feel of age, something never to be faked.

His wife bustled up, a cup of tea in her hand, and her apron pocket bulging with Georges money. "You look worried." she said.

"I am," he replied.

Her mouth made a wrinkled pout. "No need to be worried. Just another week's work. You'll soon knock up another one, won't you?"

He looked down the road that George had taken. "It's not that I'm worried about. Of course I can soon make another one. But this time I'll try to get *two* genuine drawers. That cheap veneer . . . ?" It offended him as the master craftsman he was. "Soon as it gets wet—damp even—it'll lift right off and expose the plywood underneath."

In his estate car George was singing. A half-remembered Irish song— the song of a warrior returning from the wars in triumph. Overhead it was just starting to rain.

START COUNTING

THE SOUNDPROOFING BETWEEN MY HOUSE AND my neighbour is pretty good. Occasionally you might hear an extreme sound like the scream of a child or the shatter of glass, but otherwise, nothing. Except for the bedroom adjoining mine.

Soon after moving in he lost his job poor chap, and since then they haven't really got around to doing all they intended doing; so in their bedroom is just one small square of carpet with a lot of wood floor surrounding it and, just once in a while I can hear his slow tread, or the sharp slap of her flip-flops, and some Sunday mornings the pitter patter of those tiny feet Best Men always joke about.

It is never a distinct sound, nothing annoying, nothing to complain about—on the contrary it's . . . well . . . comforting in a way, like the rumble of a distant train, reminding me that, no matter how isolated these two small houses may be at the end of their country lane, I am not entirely alone anymore.

I remember thinking that when I watched the removal van trundle up just over a year ago. The house had been empty for nearly two years and I'd got used to not worrying about what I wore, or whether I wore anything at all when pottering about in the garden! At first it seemed like an intrusion and when I saw the two children—a boy and a girl—I wasn't sure at all. Within twenty four hours I knew everything was going to work out beautifully; the kids were pleasant and well mannered and when I met Barry and Clare I knew where they got it from.

Barry comes from Acton, but should have been a Scot. Soft spoken, diffident almost, but with a kind of canny perception; slight and wiry, with not an ounce of excess fat on him, and all of it sinew and energy—the type that Gorbals' street fighters are made of and, if there happens to be a war on, end up winning an MC. Gnarled before his time it came as a small shock to learn that he was only thirty.

Clare I took to immediately. But I imagine all men do. She's as fair as Barry is dark, and a good job too because anything other than blonde and she'd be taken for a gipsy. Some women learn to project their sexuality, some never understand it at all, others merely prop it up with whatever the cosmetician or the fashion house is offering this year. Clare is a natural. She doesn't try because she doesn't have to. That doesn't mean to say she isn't aware though Yet, at first glance, all one sees is a wide mouthed, wide hipped, rather jolly girl. It is the second glance that is dangerous.

When they are home a small light burns over the porch. To light the way I suppose for any friend who might drop by. Although recently there have been very few of those.

The whole house was dark when I drove back from the station, but then I expected it to be; Barry, I knew, had gone up north to see about a possible job, and Clare had seized the opportunity, and taken the children over to see her mother. I have only met Clare's mother once, but they are two of a kind. Aware.

The day had a kind of tingle to it for me and later, much later, I found I was too revved up to do anything but lie on top of my bed in the darkness.

That's when I heard the sound. The familiar sound of footsteps from the bedroom next door. Or at least I didn't hear it—NOT right away. It had become so much a part of my pattern of life here that the sound filtered into my mind, and then just sort of lodged there for a few moments. Until I heard it again—footsteps—and suddenly realised that they were coming from an empty house.

I've been burgled once, way back before Barry and Clare moved in and I *was* living in total isolation at the end of the lane. I think that, more distressing than losing so many precious and personal things the chilling thought that I might have returned home early and walked in on . . . what? A stockinged face? A cosh?

I listened very, very intently now. I could hear my heart pounding away, but nothing else. I relaxed again, and lit another cigarette then, through the scratch of the match I again heard those footsteps. There was definitely someone moving around in Barry's house, yet, when I craned my head to look there wasn't a light showing. Someone moving about in the darkness?

I'll never know why I didn't call the police. They say that in moments of panic people do strange and unpredictable things. I dialled Barry's number. Perhaps I wanted the intruder to share my panic—the sudden, shattering ring of the phone? There is something cold and forboding about the clinical sound of a phone in an otherwise silent night. It felt odd, weird, to sit holding the receiver, hearing it buzz at my end, hearing it ring faintly, far away in the hallway of the house next door.

Do you ever catch yourself counting at times of stress? The patterns on the wallpaper? The number of panes in a window?

A dozen. I told myself I would let it ring a dozen times. Nine. Ten. Then suddenly the phone stopped ringing and the receiver was live in my hand, I waited several seconds, sure that I could hear someone breathing on the other end, and then, tentatively, "Hello?" Hallo. Hallo. Hello!

"Oh, it's you," Barry's voice was flat and matter of fact.

"Barry!"

"What can I do for you?"

"Barry, sorry to disturb you, but . . . " another kind of panic now, "I heard someone moving around, and there are no lights on, and you're supposed to be away."

"SHE thinks I'm away."

"She?"

"Clare."

"But Clare's with her mother surely?"

"That's what she'd like me to think." I could detect a slur in his voice now.

"Barry, have you been drinking?"

"On and off all day."

"What's wrong?"

125

"Nothing." There was a pause, and then he went on, "Everything's wrong."

I suddenly felt cold. And shaky. A reaction setting in, "Look I'm coming round."

"No," Barry replied, "It doesn't concern you."

"*I'm coming round.*"

The porch light went on briefly as he opened the door and I saw the tears, the pale thin face. Then the light went out again, and we stood in the shadows of the hallway. "Are we going to stay in the dark?"

"No lights," he said, "She'll see lights," he took me through to the kitchen at the back. The curtains were drawn back and it was brighter here; I could see the whisky bottle on the table, and the shotgun lying next to it. He saw me looking at it and picked it up, "You won't stop me," he said, and wandered away to sit heavily in a chair, the shotgun across his knees, "She's a cow." He played with the safety catch of the gun, pushing it up and back, up and back. Eleven times I counted him do that. "I phoned her mother, asked to talk to her." He stared at me, and I could now see a spasm of muscle, a nervous tic below his eye, "She told me Clare was in bed asleep, with a headache. *With a headache!* They're two of a kind, her and her mother." He put the gun between his knees and leaned his chin on the barrels, "It's the same, old story as before." He told me then. About Clare. The infidelities, the affairs—the last so tempestuous it had cost him his job—the lies and bitterness and cheating. None of it was really a surprise to me. When he'd finished, he sat for a long moment looking at nothing in particular. I really felt sorry for him. Then, "This time I've had it. This time I'll be waiting for her." I wondered why he was so sure she was having an affair. He told me. The month before he had again gone chasing after a job up North, and again she had taken the children to her mother's. "But she came back here and spent the night with a man." Subtle things only a jealous husband might notice; a crumpled nightdress, a cigarette end, hair in a basin, but most of all Clare's attitude, taunting and triumphant, "She has to let me know you see, without actually telling me, she has to let me know."

I tried to dissuade him. He was imagining things, misinterpreting, and after all, if Clare had brought someone home, surely I, living right next door . . . ? He shook his head, "She's too damned clever, probably brought him in over the fields," he took a swig from the bottle, "Well this time I'M the clever one." He patted the shotgun, "This time I'm ready."

I forced a smile, "You can't really mean that, Barry. It's so . . . *French.* The wife and her lover . . . "

"Oh I've got nothing against him, he's a nice enough chap." I've often read 'profound shock', but never properly experienced it before, "You know who it is?"

Barry nodded, "I've seen them together a couple of times, holding hands, and once kissing."

"But you couldn't have done. I mean, how *could* you have done?"

The spasm returned to his face, "It wasn't easy. I nearly went for her then. But I wasn't ready then. "Anyway, in the middle of a super-market . . . ?"

"A supermarket?" I was lost. "That young fellow, well he can't be more than 25, under manager or something. He's the one."

I was getting things into perspective now, "You've seen them?"

"Several times," Barry replied, "As I've said, I've got nothing against him. I know how Clare works. If she wants something she gets it, what-ever."

More and more into perspective, "When did you see them together, Barry?"

He shrugged, "Last week was the last time, but it's been going on for a lot longer."

"I see." And I really did. I'd never noticed before that the tiles in Barry's kitchen were in neat rows of twelve.

"What will you do now?" I became aware of him again, aware of the gun now pointing at me, "Will you warn her? Stop her?" I stood up and the gun followed me, "I don't know, Barry. Warn her? No, I won't do that."

I carefully made my way into the hall. Barry followed me, "Perhaps I'm wrong. I hope I'm wrong, but if she DOES come back here tonight, well . . . I'll know won't I?" I opened the door and turned to look at him. He sat down on the stairs facing the door, and cocked the hammers of the shotgun, "That's fair," I said, "That's leaving it to fate," I pushed the door wider.

"You don't think she will come back here tonight, do you?" said Barry.

"Frankly, Barry," I replied, "At this moment I don't know what to think."

By the time I got back to my house I did. I opened the sitting room door very gently and just stood there, looking. Clare was exactly as I had left her . . . what . . . three hours ago? Sprawled across the deep sofa, her naked body pale and luscious. Her lips were parted and she was snoring ever so slightly; the month before when I had sat up in her bed and watched, and listened to her snore, it had struck me as enchanting, a human frailty necessary in one so perfect. Now it seemed vaguely repellant. I noticed too that ugly bruise on her thigh, and remembered her laughing explanation that she had 'bumped into something in the super-market'.

I moved to stand over her and touch her for the last time. It meant nothing, and I shook her awake.

She stared at me through sleep and opened her arms to embrace me again, her breath was sickly sour. I stepped back, "You have to go." Only half awake as she was, I don't know what she made of my explanation that a stranded friend had called, and was coming to stay, and she couldn't possibly be found here. But it didn't really matter, did it?

The last I saw of her she was tousle haired, half dressed and stumbling—looking for all the world like some doxy who had just been wrestling in the hay with some super-market under manager or whatever.

I stood by the window and counted off her footsteps along the short path. Eight. Just eight. And then of course she was at her own front door.

LITTLE BROWN MEN

1 HAVE ALWAYS BEEN ONE FOR THE TRADITIONAL ENGLISH
breakfast; not just the eggs and bacon but also the kedgeree, the
haddock and best of all the succulent kidneys. I was the one who found
Tony's body and I haven't been able to touch kidneys since.

We were never able to determine whether they had roasted his testi-
cles while they were still attached to his body or not, but certainly they
were not attached to him when I found him in that dark little back
room we always used for our clandestine meetings.

Nor could we understand why they had committed such a heinous
act against Tony because he was not a member of The Service, merely a
from time to time useful informant. He was not at all vital. No, it was
the fact that they knew about him and where to find him that had us
worried. It was a clear breach of security, and security was uppermost in
our minds at that particular time because, just a few days hence, we were
to cover the visit of a Very Important Person who, should he be assassinated whilst on our soil, under OUR jurisdiction, would lead to all sorts
of embarrassment, lots of paper work, a general air of despondency and
perhaps even cancellation of all summer leave. And I had already
booked the villa in Marbella. Close to the Golf Course.

My first action was to consult with Kart, my opposite number in the
KGB. Kart, or to give him his full name, Kartovski, and me are the very
best of tenuous enemies. Where diplomacy and détente failed the

Niblick and the putter triumphed, we are both very keen golfers. As I expected, Kart hotly denied having anything to do with Tony and what's more he was very indignant, after all we knew his methods—perhaps an eye gouging, a little ear chopping, or even a red hot iron on the soles of the feet, but never, never THAT, I believed him, and we fell into serious discussion—mostly about Nicklaus who was looking very good in The Open at that time. Later, as I was leaving, Kart grabbed my arm and, in a surfeit of Vodka and those little green apples you are supposed to bite into between each gulp, and which are supposed to keep you sober, and probably do if you limit your consumption to no more than four bottles, he told me what I had really come there to hear, Something Of Importance, "Ninotchka," he said, (He WAS very drunk, even by his standards), "Ninotchka, it is our fault," I waited, and eventually he continued, "I've taught them too well, guided them," I wondered if a quick eye witness's resume of his play from the 15th at Wentworth last Tuesday might jolt him out of it, but then he hiccuped and went on, "The little brown men."

I felt a shiver go up my back and thought that if I phoned right away I might at least get my deposit back on the villa in Marbella, "The little brown men" could mean any one of the half hundred or so emergent nations so recently erupted across Africa, and the leaders of which, having put down the thigh bone of their enemy had bit instead into democracy, and found it tasted so much better. The little brown men who, in between awarding themselves OBE's, VC's, Garters (and once, to my eternal amusement, the MCC), presented the most salient threat to our V.I.P. I descended to base tactics and offered Kart a stroke a hole when next we met; he wavered, his eyes glazed, but I saw it was no good, he was at root a dedicated patriot, Mother Russia, The Party, The Cause were inviolable. And I finally had to concede TWO strokes a hole.

Even then he didn't tell me that much, just rumour and hearsay that someone amongst the little brown men had come up with a new and brilliant scheme to penetrate our security, filch our secrets—and kill our V.I.P.

As I putted down the corridors of power that evening I knew it had shaken me; even where the carpet extended to the Director's door, and where I always got a birdy, I muffed it.

I knew too that The Director was equally as shaken as I; par to the door of the lift is an easy (to my mind) three. He was two over par at the halfway stage, and his final putt missed the propped bowler hat altogether.

As I thought again of the little brown men I feared for the future; if it went on like this I might find my handicap up to seven.

"Wainwright," as soon as The Director said the name I realized he was absolutely right. Apart from me only Wainwright had known about Tony and where he lived. Wainwright was the key.

Wainwright is a tanned and handsome man, erudite and intelligent with three superb children and a wife who ranks amongst the most beautiful women I have ever seen. I envy Wainwright because the grounds of his wonderful house run right down to one of the best golf courses in the county. They held the most exciting major tournament of the season there last year, and when I excitedly asked Wainwright if he had seen Trevino drive that miraculous winning drive from the 18th (which is just the other side of Wainwright's hedge), he said no, then winked and explained that his wife had just come back after a two months absence that day, and the children had been away, and ... I wouldn't say Wainwright was perverted exactly, but you have to admit, a bit strange.

It took me quite a while to get to Wainwright's house, mainly because the last mile or so of road runs very close to the course, and the pro there is first class and well worth a watch.

Wainwright opened the door to me, and lead me through to his oak beaded study. He knew why I was there and we sat and discussed the possibilities; he was adamant that he kept no secret papers at the house and that, on the rare occasions when he had phoned Tony, he always made sure that he was completely alone. It was about then that I noticed the little brown man sitting, watching us!

A very little brown man indeed, about five or six years old I thought, with eyes like big luminous saucers and a smile curved to fit a watermelon, an oddly wise and wrinkled little face. He had wandered in through the French doors while we had been talking, and now he resumed the business in hand, scrummaged around under the sofa, found his ball, and went out into the garden again. My suspicions were aroused, where there is little brown child there inevitably has to be a little brown father. Wainwright smiled away my fears; there were several black children at the local school for infants—and that is where Wainwright's infant was going until it (or was it she?)

131

reached the tender age of seven, when it would be whisked away to a prep school as the first stepping stone to a private and more superior education. Meanwhile Wainwright's own daughter was encouraged along the paths of equality, liberalism and emancipation—apart from which she rather liked the little black boy.

Wainwright grinned, "One or other of his parents comes to collect him every afternoon, but they never come further than the main gate, just stand there and call out his name—'Lusitania'."

Lusitania? Wainwright grinned again, "I have a feeling they thought it was a king." Lusitania! Then I saw the funny side and wondered if Lusitania had a sister . . . ship. Titanic perhaps? "Why, man, you all know she always suffers from that sinking feeling!" I felt elated for a moment—then got that sinking feeling myself, Wainwright had given me no hope, no clue at all.

As I left I patted Lusitania on his smoke stack.

Our V.I.P. arrived and the next couple of days were desperate. The V.I.P., a little brown man himself (well, more burnt sienna actually) wanted to 'meet, and get to the very heart of the people'. I suspected that some of the people wanted to get to his heart too—preferably with a soft nosed .44.

It was going to be very, very difficult. Our V.I.P. was terribly aware of his image and awfully miffed when we got him into his hotel not exactly up the back stairs in a sack, but certainly unobtrusively.

He had worn his special Chief of the Imperial Staff uniform too; this was an unusual garment, like a tri-colour made from vertical strips of khaki, navy and air force blue so that, depending upon which angle you viewed him from, he was a General, an Admiral or an Air Vice-Marshal. I noticed that he wore the Croix de Guerre over his heart and politely asked that he award himself the Iron Cross First Class instead because, being of German manufacture, it stood a better chance of resisting a high velocity bullet.

It was clear from the outset that there was going to be a conflict of interest; he favoured spending his time addressing the masses from his balcony, whereas we had something more in mind like locking him in a tin box and depositing it in a bank vault; that first evening we compromised and he attended a dinner at which the only guest who wasn't a member of The Service was the Foreign Secretary and, remembering Suez, we even frisked him. The waiters too were Service members, you could tell the way they spilled the soup weighted down as they were by their Magnums. Not of Champagne!

I was in charge of security so obviously devoted all my energies to it; I even pondered the problem to the extent that, when playing round my home course at Richmond, I actually found myself bunkered twice. I was beginning to hate our V.I.P.

The various Embassy junkets were comparatively easy to secure but the big, bad one was looming up; the climax of his visit was to be a 'walkabout'. That in itself is liable to make a man lose his grip—or at least change the position of his hands—but worse still the intended walkabout was to take place in a certain area of London where Tarzan would have felt at home; seething with little brown men.

I tackled the problem like a military operation, I meticulously, and personally investigated every approach—I had come unstuck once before you see, not investigating every approach, and as a result The Captain's Challenge Cup now resides on another's mantle shelf.

Finally I called a special meeting of my elite, on the 15th green at Weybridge. It is especially suited for that purpose because the fairway is wide and open and the nearest real cover is a good two shot away (Although Tammy Hepworth once accomplished it in one but that was pure fluke). It so happened that Kart was holding his regular 'recovery of dissidents' meeting on the 14th and although I could not clearly see his face, I knew he was looking my way and commiserating, and glad that it wasn't his problem.

I told my elite about the rumour, about the little brown men who might, just might, have come up with something new and deadly, and that we had to be very, very alert. They were all of them keyed up and tensed, and shuffled their plimsolled feet. I always insist that they wear plimsolls on these occasions because I am often a guest at the club and have had some memorable long putts on the 15th, and anyway the green-keeper is a good friend of mine.

I had decided on an unprecedented step, and one that was to impose the greatest strain upon the resources of The Service.

I have been to Africa several times and know its dangers (Slice from the 12th tee on Table Mountain and your ball ends up in the ocean)—and I also know its terrain, the veldt, the bush, the jungle, I have been hopelessly lost in them all, so, working on the premis that the unfamiliar looks all the same, I had decided to rig the V.I.P.'S walkabout. He would actually only walk in and around three streets in a very confined and pre-planned area and, after he left one area, my men would change the street signs, perhaps bring in a false post box or other salient landmark, and, hopefully, he would never know the difference. This masterful plan of mine would enable me to do three vitally important things; seal off the walkabout area; frisk and clear everyone within it; and put the whole damned thing into my aide's hands so I could get back to my challenge game against Forteseue—he had taken a tenner off me last time and I was eager for revenge.

The walkabout was set for a Saturday and I prayed for rain; rain would at least keep a few of them away. The last time I can remember such a hot and sunny Saturday was when Palmer pipped Gary Player. They were out early, in droves, and at the various entrances to the predetermined area, my men were hard pressed checking everyone through, but they did a marvellous and thorough job and then, after the V.I.P.'s limousined entourage had passed through, they closed the barriers tight.

The V.I.P. alighted to a wave of cheers and enthusiasm; he made a very impressive sight, having chosen to wear a 'native', traditional costume' which, I suspect Hardy Amies might have had a hand in, he wore a full lion skin with the head and upper jaw as a kind of hat, it did tend to make him look a bit like an African version of Jonah but nevertheless it was impressive I suppose, especially to a lioness.

I accompanied him every step of the way, and for a while all went well, there were a few snags of course, there always are; once when Simkins hastily put up a fresh street sign and got it upside down, but our V.I.P. did not appear to notice and it only served to confirm my suspicion that he could not read. And once when I came face to face with Eggerton who, in his enthusiasm to merge, had actually blacked up his face. I know Eggerton's penchant for amateur theatricals—and indeed once had had to sit through a very wobbly Oklahoma—and hoped he would keep himself in check and not sink to one knee and give a rendering of 'Mammy', but apart from that it all went very well indeed. The V.I.P. stopped and chatted to this person and that, and patted the heads of children and got very hot indeed and, I am sure, regretted the lion skin bitterly, wishing perhaps that he might have settled for just a pair of snakeskin shoes.

After the third trip around the same area he DID seem to get a bit baffled when he kept seeing the same faces, and I realised too late that to HIM, they did NOT look all alike. I covered it nicely though, muttering something about, "They follow their spiritual leader everywhere." At one point the V.I.P. stopped and talked to a young woman who stood very straight and tall indeed, as though she had only just taken the bale off her head, and she laughed a lot and showed beautifully straight and white teeth, and her ample breasts, that looked like mudhuts blown over in a strong wind, jiggled provocatively. I had eventually to remind the V.I.P. that there was still much to see (The first street for the fourth time), and he moved on, but I glanced back and saw his aide—de-camp now talking to her, and writing something down in a little note book. Then immediately afterwards my own men moving in to grab her (Robinson a bit too enthusiastically I thought) and hustle her away for further investigation. Well, those mudhuts MIGHT have been bombs.

We came now to the pre-arranged place where he would address 'the people'. I had thought this might take anything from an hour upwards and had indeed cancelled my golf lesson at Harrods in anticipation. Surprisingly the speech was quite short; perhaps the lion skin was becoming too much, or he had remembered more pressing business of State back at his own Embassy—the young woman, cleared by my men now, had been put into the third of the limousines.

He spoke briefly and succinctly, spoke of 'pushing the white man from my country', which was a bit inaccurate because just six months before he HAD pushed the Russians out—but then pushed us in. He spoke of 'a deep mistrust of the black man for the white' which I thought unfair, in view of the fact that he does trust the Swiss white with all his money.

He finished his speech in a great welter of applause, and an even greater stamping of feet, a big rythmic sound, and I glanced at the sky and wondered if they would bring rain, and thought where were they when I needed them.

That's when it happened.

A little brown girl ducked under the wooden barrier, evaded the half hearted, desultory grasp of a policeman, and came running towards the V.I.P. She was tiny, appeared to be no more than five or six, and wore a sparkling pink dress with matching ribbons at her pigtails, a latter day Topsy who carried a big, untidy bunch of flowers for her lion clad hero.

I moved as though to stop her, but the V.I.P. shouldered me away, quickly glanced and found the nearest photographer, presented his best side to the camera and then crouched to welcome the charming child, smiling broadly like the Big Black Father. She in turn stretched up and lifted her bouquet. I kicked her at the base of the spine knocking her face down, then aimed my second kick at her kidneys, perhaps I was remembering poor Tony then.

Only those very nearby saw the automatic fall out of her bouquet and the subsequent rioting continued into the night and well into the next day before the police were able to quell it.

It had been something about the way she had carried the bouquet, and her general gait, not the hop step of a child; her face too, like Lusitania's had had that wise beyond its years, old before its time look.

Why on earth had we always and only thought of the 'little brown men' as African? You get little brown men in New Guinea too. And pigmies.

It was unmitigated disaster, of course; oh not our V.I.P., we sent him back all in one piece, I escaped the wrath of the rioters too, my men had closed ranks around me and hustled me into one of the limousines.

No, it was that second kick I aimed at that thirty year old 'child'.

The little bugger bit my leg and The Captain's Challenge Cup again resides on the mantle shelf of another.

As Custom Would Have It

I FIRST SAW MARYANNE LOOKING SLIGHTLY BLURRED, upside down and with a feint cross accurately marking her delectable navel, I'm a fashion photographer and although most of my work these days is done out of a studio, on 35mm, with a Nikon, I still occasionally use the wonderful old plate camera my father gave me. In the main for special advertising shots where composition is very important and, inverted or not, the image on the ground glass screen makes life a whole lot easier.

I was still in the embryo stages of lining up my shot, and the two models I had hired were relaxed, laughing and talking, and that's when Maryanne walked in. She was working in the studio next door, knew one of my girls and had popped in to say hello, wearing a big, brilliant white smile and very little else.

I meet and work with, and frequently enjoy many beautiful women in my job; possibly some of the most beautiful women in the world. I thought I had got used to seeing them. Until I met Maryanne; she was stunning. Tall, slim as a reed, small nosed and wide mouthed, with intensely flashing eyes that were just a shade or three darker than her own glorious skin. Yes, she was black, a Zulu, and later I found out, a real Zulu princess, and there was something magical about her, truly magical. Like any thoroughbred she was delicately fine, so that she seemed to have the best of European features, and the best of

African, delightfully blended to make me fall in love with her at first sight.

It was a meeting of souls too, her English was utterly perfect and as soon as I started talking to her I found that we had so many interests in common; riding, tennis, the same tastes in food, films, theatre.

I took her out that same evening, and then every evening for nearly a month, and never once tired of looking at her, being with her, listening, enchanted, to her musical laughter. I had had several coloured girl friends before and always found that they had a gaiety, a warm enthusiasm, an almost childlike *attack* on life that one never found in European girls. Maryanne was like that, but much, much more; there was a sort of spirituality about her, an overwhelming sense of kindness that wasn't, but was close to, mother love.

I didn't take her to bed, not because I didn't want her, I DID want her desperately, but somehow it didn't matter just then, her presence was enough. Also I had decided to marry her and just once in my young life I really wanted to do the right thing.

I'm usually a 'one supper and you're mine' kind of chap—well, who isn't these days?—and I must say that it felt odd wanting her so badly and yet resisting my own desires. Odd, but right. Honourable. Maryanne understood that because, as I got to know her better I got to know of her family, and her upbringing until she was nearly ten. It was like something out of a very old book; mud huts, a proper chief-tain, a witch doctor, an almost primeval protocol, but best of all, a community. "If someone had a pig, then we all ate pork," she would tell me, "and if a neighbour died, we all grieved," and then, looking shyly at me, "and if a girl friend married, everyone was happy."

There were passionate times, of course, times when I came very close to not doing the right thing. She was terrific, there WAS an innocence about her, and I believed her when she told me that she had never really, properly known a man. At the same time though she could be a tiger, fantastic, instinctively responding to me and yet still malleable. Still with much to learn. And on the other side of the coin, before I would drop her at her door and lightly kiss her, she could be so very tender.

On the anniversary of our first meeting one month before, I asked her to marry me, and she accepted.

I must confess I had a moment of trepidation when I told my parents, but I should have had more faith in Maryanne; she cast one of her spells on them and they, like me, fell in love with her immediately.

It was a church wedding, my parents wanted that, and so, curiously enough, did I. Maryanne didn't wear white, but a wonderful cream dress; I jokingly told her that it made her look like the most delicious cup of coffee any man could ever want. None of her family were there and we were both very sad about that; but her father had got himself involved on the periphery of politics and the ghastly archaic South African government would allow none of the family exit permits. Her friends however turned out in droves and it was the wedding of the year in that quiet little Sussex village. Maryanne was intensely interested in the ceremony; she had read it through a dozen times and during the actual wedding itself she followed the vicar's every word with great concentration. I suppose, the whole of her early life being one long ceremonial, it had an even deeper than usual significance for her.

We honeymooned on the Algarve, in a villa just outside Faro and overlooking a wild, unspoiled beach. We would swim in the sea during the day and sit on the beach and crack and eat charcoaled shellfish with our fingers. And in the evening we would swim naked in the villa's secluded pool, drink ice cold Vino Verde, and of course, make love.

Once we drove inland then stopped and walked through the dusty fields adjoining a small village; it was a place I had been to before because many women work in the fields and some of them enjoy a brief but magnificent beauty, tall, dark eyed girls, their backs held straight by a fierce peasant pride and they had provided me with a folio of photographs that had won many prizes. Maryanne walked amongst them wearing, as many models do when not modelling, the very simplest of garments, a straight shift in plain hopsack that eddied around her, and sometimes clung provocatively to her in an Atlantic breeze. She was like a peasant girl herself, a child of the earth, of Nature.

That evening as we sat around the pool I noticed that she was again reading the wedding ceremony. I teased her about it, was she tired of me already and looking for a loophole? But she was very serious, the words were very important she said, "love, honour, . . . until death," it was as complete as the ceremony she might have had in her own village back home. Almost.

Almost? She stared into my eyes, "You have given me your name, your protection, your promise, now I must give YOU something." I kissed her breasts and said she already had, but she pushed me away for a moment and said she wanted us to be complete, she wanted to make a sacrifice. I still teased her, should I rush out and get a chicken or a goat? "I give you part of my life," she said, "So that you may live longer." It was so charming, so movingly simple. She kissed the tears from my cheek; and I from hers.

We had planned to live in my bachelor flat for at least another year while we looked around and found exactly the right house, but when, just three months later, Maryanne announced that she was pregnant, the whole process had to be speeded up. Neverthe-less we did find exactly the right house, on the fringe of Bayswater, tall and Georgian with a splendid garden. It was there, in the big bedroom overlooking the front that Maryanne presented me with our first born, Nicholas. There hadn't been time to get her to the hospital, and anyway the doctor said he had never seen such an easy or natural birth, "Just joy, no fear to tighten the muscles."

If before our marriage had been pure bliss then the arrival of our son turned it into a minor miracle. I know that many of my friends—knowing me, but not Maryanne well enough—had mentally given it a year or two. Instead it grew stronger, we loved each other more each day not less, and when four years after Nicholas, Maryanne presented me with Sara, that seemed to consolidate the whole fantastic relationship, I think, if I was honest with myself there was a bit of ego, a hint of reflected glory about it; it really was something to go somewhere, anywhere with Maryanne and sense the approval. It was nice too to look across a crowded room and see the most beautiful woman there and know she was mine.

It was just one week before our tenth wedding anniversary that I went back to the Algarve again. Alone this time because Maryanne did not like the idea of relinquishing the children to an au pair for more than a day or two, and frankly neither did I. Anyway I would 'be very busy working'. It was my agent's idea to go back and do a follow up to the folio that had been so very successful so long before, a kind of 'where are they now?' feature.

The first thing I did on landing in Faro was to buy Maryanne's anniversary present; an exquisitely tooled silver and onyx bracelet with the simplicity of design I knew she liked so much.

The next day I walked those dusty fields again. I carried a copy of my original folio and, with the aid of an interpreter, tried to run down the original models. It was a very depressing experience; several had died, and most of the others had changed almost beyond recognition. Hard work, privation and perhaps something in-bred had taken a terrible toll.

Those fair cheeks of not so very long before had lost that silky, brushed-olive texture, and were now wrinkled and prune-like; slim hips had become gross, pert breasts were now pendulous.

I was reminded of the butterfly with its short life span, its painfully brief flirtation with beauty. I got some terrific pictures though.

It was on the plane back that I thought about age. Life so far had ticked by so easily and happily that I had never really thought about it before. I was thirty nine, and in a few months time I would be forty, on the brink of middle-age. Yet I still felt like a young stallion, still felt no more than twenty something at least. I embarrassed myself by getting up and going to the lavatory and looking at myself in the mirror; a tanned, taut face topped with a full head of hair looked back at me, I wrinkled my eyes in mirthless laughter and then in repose moved even closer to the mirror, the laugh lines had been momentary, now there was no sign of them. I not only still FELT young, I still looked it. I returned to my seat and was about to order a large Scotch, but then settled for an orange juice instead.

Maryanne was out collecting the children from school when I got back, and I must confess that I again went and looked at myself in the mirror, the full length, brilliantly lit bathroom mirror this time. I stripped to my pants then turned this way and that but saw only firm muscle, and a youthful, unlined face.

I don't know what Maryanne made of that meeting. Nicholas and Sara came running at me, and I picked them up, one in each arm and did not hear their eager greeting because I was staring at Maryanne. I saw the beginning of the crow's feet around her eyes, the hint of the long line running vertically down each cheek, the pucker around the lips that now seemed thinner than before. When she moved towards me too, I noticed that she did not hold herself as proud and straight as once had been, there was a roundness about her shoulders and a tired quality in her movement. I quickly kissed her then held her close and saw the silver strands in her hair. Her body no longer felt slim against me, her belly was not firm anymore. Under those rounded shoulders I could barely feel the fine bones. For a moment I could not remember, her exact age . . . she had been twenty two when I married her . . . ten years . . . she was only thirty two now! And already on her way to becoming an old woman.

That evening it had been my plan to take her out to meet an American friend who had just arrived in town, but I called and cancelled; I told him and Maryanne that I was too tired after my journey.

I spent most of the next day in my dark room, processing the shots I had taken in Portugal. As I washed each print, another, then another lined and aged face would loom up at me; a gallery of hags. I thought then of the various trips I had made across the world; to Japan, India, and even the peasant villages of Italy and Greece. I thought of how many of the women of those countries suddenly, almost over-night, aged. And I thought again of Maryanne.

We went out together only a few times over the next few weeks, and then always to the discreet restaurants with dark and shadowy alcove tables. We made love only sporadically and always, at my insistence, with the lights out. One morning however, I awoke first and Maryanne was still deep in sleep and I lightly stripped back the bedclothes and looked at her.

The early morning sun was harsh and showed the deepening lines across her face and whole body, showed the veining and puckering of flesh.

I worked more and more at my studio now, later and later. And then I met Sylvie. She was blonde and vivacious. Nineteen. And British. Her wicked sense of fun appealed to me and as I was working on a whole fashion spread with Sylvie the model, we saw a great deal of each other.

One day, about a week after meeting her, I took her to lunch and she prattled away in her childish way and made me laugh a lot. It was she who suggested that I might take her out that evening, I hesitated but then finally agreed and made an excuse to Maryanne and picked Sylvia up at her Chelsea flat at eight. I took her to a new restaurant—well, new to me, but not to Sylvie. I liked it, it was garish and wildly over-lit and we had a prominent table overlooking the dance floor and I noticed a lot of young men looking at Sylvie. Then later I suggested that we dance she laughed and said, "Not here. NOBODY dances HERE," and we should go to a disco. I protested, I said a disco was for kids and she frowned at me and said, "Well, you're not exactly an old man, are you?"

and when asked to guess my age, said I looked no more than twenty nine, I was beginning to like Sylvie a great deal.

We went to the disco and I had a great time, and the next day I went to get myself a new hairstyle and buy myself some new clothes; a very slim-fitting single breasted suit in pale lemon, like all the kids were wearing. A few days later I traded in my little Italian saloon car for a drop head sports, it wasn't quite so useful for ferrying my equipment around in, but it made me feel good.

I took up tennis again, and found I hadn't lost my touch, I was beating boys who were half my age, I had joined a gym too, and all that exercise was doing me good, I actually felt younger; the man who gave me my regular facial said I must be Peter Pan, he had less and less to do on me each day.

I was running out of excuses for Maryanne; not that she said very much. She just followed me with those big, dark eyes of hers, wondering, I could hardly bear to look at her these days, not just out of guilt but also because, the ageing process having touched her seemed now to speed up, to accelerate. Her face was heavily lined now, and she was carrying a great deal too much weight. It was as though she had given up caring.

I was having an affair with Sylvie now and that wasn't terrific but it was pretty good. What I enjoyed most was taking her out, being seen around with her and, my mind made up now, introducing her to my friends. Sometimes I'd catch sight of the two of us in a mirror together and we looked so *right*. Complimentary.

Maryanne didn't understand at first and I suddenly realised that, despite the many excuses, despite the complete cessation of anything physical between us, she hadn't suspected. She really did not know.

It was harrowing to have to explain to her my feelings, and that I wanted a divorce. She said nothing, but then hurried away to the bedroom and I thought she had gone off to cry, but then she came back and she still had that scrap of paper with the wedding ceremony printed on it, all thumbed and faded now, and she put it down between us and then picked out certain lines, "Till death us do part," she was confused, a child again as she asked me how such an oath could not be binding. I explained to her that it was just a bunch of words, an oath that could be broken.

She sat back and rocked on her haunches, "No, no, no," she moaned, "Forever and ever, forever and ever, it *has* to be." My only way out, of getting through to her was to get angry, I said nothing as forever, need not be forever. She stared at me and said, "In my country it would be."

"But we are not in your country," I replied, "And that is the way of things."

She understood now, at last, and she stood up and she seemed proud and tall again, as when I had first met her, "In that case" she said, "I take back MY oath too," and she turned and walked away.

I moved in with Sylvie and put the whole thing in the hands of my solicitors. As the guilty party I did not have to appear in court and so I did not see Maryanne again for nearly a year.

Sylvie had dragged me to yet another disco, one I particularly disliked because the lighting there was very harsh and unflattering.

We had been on the floor a couple of times and I was seated again getting my breath back when I saw Maryanne. At first I thought it was a trick of that horrendous lighting, or perhaps my eyes playing me up (just lately I have had a bit of trouble seeing things clearly in mid-distance), but then she moved nearer and I saw her. It was just like that first time eleven (was it really eleven!?) years ago when she had first swum into my vision. She was tall and slender as ever before, proud and upright. She must have been working very hard to get her figure back, and she had been successful. Her make-up too, I couldn't see just what she was wearing but it was damned skilful because there was now no hint of the crow's feet or wrinkles. Then she saw me, and our eyes met very briefly and I was aware, for one last time of the magic in them. Then she was screened from sight by two or three of the many young men now surrounding her and seeking her attention. Young men who must have been years younger than her, and yet she merged with them without looking at all at variance.

I stood up abruptly, and Sylvie glared at me as she had glared at me a lot of late; it was my intention to stride over and take Maryanne's hand, take her out of that group of admirers and say "You're mine. SHE is mine," but then I thought about the oath I had broken, and hers broken in return and knew that it would be no use.

I sat down again and I felt the breathlessness and palpitations return, I looked at the dark brown spots on the backs of my gnarling hands, and wondered if my toupee was on straight.